Alfred Sereno Hudson

Commemorative of Calvin and Luther Blanchard

Alfred Sereno Hudson

Commemorative of Calvin and Luther Blanchard

ISBN/EAN: 9783337126841

Printed in Europe, USA, Canada, Australia, Japan

Cover: Foto ©Andreas Hilbeck / pixelio.de

More available books at **www.hansebooks.com**

COMMEMORATIVE

OF

Calvin and Luther Blanchard

ACTON MINUTE-MEN

1775

BY

ALFRED SERENO HUDSON

AUTHOR OF

" History of Sudbury," "Annals of Sudbury, Wayland and Maynard," "Souvenir of the Wayside Inn," Etc.

PUBLISHED BY

LUKE BLANCHARD, WEST ACTON, MASS.

1899

To

THE DESCENDANTS OF THE MINUTE-MEN,

WHO, TRUE TO THEIR NAME,

MUSTERED AT THE MIDNIGHT ALARM AND

MET THE MINISTERIAL TROOPS ON APRIL 19TH, 1775,

THIS BOOK IS RESPECTFULLY INSCRIBED

BY THE PUBLISHER,

LUKE BLANCHARD, OF ACTON, MASS.,

A GRANDSON OF CALVIN

AND GRAND-NEPHEW OF LUTHER BLANCHARD.

CONTENTS.

LIST OF ILLUSTRATIONS.

DESCRIPTION OF ILLUSTRATIONS.

THE START FOR CONCORD.

The picture of Captain Isaac Davis leading his company of minute-men from his house, April 19th, 1775, is reproduced from a painting by Mr. Arthur F. Davis. The picture is considered natural.

THE OLD NORTH BRIDGE, CONCORD, MASS.

The author of this book, in making a picture of the Old North Bridge and the Major Buttrick house on the hill, has followed the suggestions of a picture by Doolittle and Earle, made about three months after the Concord fight; while for the adjacent country he has followed nature as it is at the present time, which is, probably, in its main features, about as it was in 1775. The ground on the northerly side of the bridge about the causeway is low, and at high water the river sometimes overflowed it. The causeway was short, and turned easterly by the upland, and entered the highway which led to the neighborhood of Major Buttrick's house. The point of view from which the picture was taken is on the southerly side of the river, a few rods above the bridge.

THE JONATHAN HOSMER HOUSE.

The picture of this house was sketched by the author, from a description given him by Mrs. Emeline Hall of West Acton, Mass., a granddaughter of Deacon Jonathan Hosmer. Mrs. Hall was born in the old Hosmer house in 1868, and lived there till she was eighteen years old. Her recollection of the house is quite distinct, and when the drawing was completed, she pronounced it natural. There formerly stood to the westerly of the house a shed and chaise-house; and a barn stood on the opposite side of the road. The tree on the south-easterly corner was an elm, and in the rear were several butternut trees. The house faced southerly. The front yard was large and unfenced. The present road from West Acton to South Acton was not in existence in 1775. The old road from Acton center, so much as is represented in the picture, is the same now, as formerly, and runs by the memorial stone, joining the West and South Acton road, nearly opposite the Herman A. Gould house. Formerly this road turned at a point near the Hosmer house, and went up the hill northerly of the present South Acton road; this latter section can still be traced by a cart-path. The front room to the south-westerly, which was entered by the side door, was used for the kitchen.

PREFACE.

In writing this little volume the author has taken such liberty as he considered suitable and the nature of the case required. There has been but little consultation with the publisher as to what matter it should contain, or the form of its presentation ; his purpose being to have properly given an account of the events of the first " Patriots' Day," as they stand related to the dedication of the " Memorial Stone " erected by him to the memory of his ancestor, Calvin Blanchard, and his great uncle, Luther ; a purpose commendable in itself, and in the interest of local history. Whatever relates to the publisher personally has been editorially inserted, and in no instance has any part of the manuscript been submitted for his perusal. As the work has been gotten up by the publisher for private distribution, the subject is more specific, and its scope more limited than if it were a contribution to literature of a more public character.

It is, nevertheless, the hope of the author that these few pages may prove a fresh inspiration to all who are interested in what " Patriots' Day " is suggestive of, and may tend to increase the admiration of posterity for the work and character of the Minute-men of '75.

A. S. H.

AYER, MASS., June 8, 1899.

"But, O where can dust to dust
    Be consigned so well,
As where heaven its dews shall shed,
On the martyred patriot's bed,
And the rocks shall raise their head,
    Of his deeds to tell?"

Pierpont.

HONOR TO WHOM HONOR IS DUE.

I.

At Acton, Middlesex County, Massachusetts, April 19th, 1895, a memorial stone was dedicated with the following inscription:

"FROM THIS FARM WENT
CALVIN AND LUTHER BLANCHARD
TO CONCORD FIGHT AND BUNKER HILL,
SONS OF SIMON BLANCHARD, WHO WAS
KILLED AT THE BATTLE OF QUEBEC, 1759.
LUTHER WAS THE FIRST MAN HIT BY A
BRITISH BULLET AT THE OLD NORTH BRIDGE
AND DIED IN THE SERVICE OF HIS COUNTRY
A FEW MONTHS LATER."

This memorial was erected by Luke Blanchard of Acton, a grand-son of Calvin and grand-nephew of Luther, whose names are thereon inscribed; and is situated in that part of the town which is known as West Acton, about one mile northerly of the Fitchburg railroad station and about two miles from Acton Center.

The stone stands by the wayside, in a quiet spot, and at a junction of roads, one of which leads to South Acton, the other northerly towards the center.

The farm on which the monument stands is now known as the Hermon A. Gould farm, but more than a century ago it was a part of the homestead of Jonathan Hosmer. The dedicatory exercises consisted of patriotic speeches, appro-priate music and prayer; and to preserve some of these for the perusal of posterity, as well as to present some additional facts relative to the notable lives and events thus com-memorated, is the object of the following compilation. Be-fore entering upon the task allotted us, it may be appropriate to remark, that it is a delicate one to undertake, from the fact that the hero of our sketch had many peers, and space forbids an extended mention of all of them.

While there went from Acton to the North Bridge at Concord, Luther Blanchard, the fifer, there went also Isaac Davis, Abner Hosmer and James Hayward. These, with their fellow townsmen who went with them, all marched through a gateway of glory, and each was a willing sacrifice ready to be offered when the time should come. There was no difference whatever in the purity of purpose that moved these young patriots; all had like hopes and like fears, and of them it could truthfully be said,

"Few were the numbers they could boast
But every freeman was a host,
And felt as if himself were he
On whose sole arm hung victory."

As of Acton, so it was of other towns.   Among these soldiers was no priority of merit.   It was a hero's day for them all.   Never since the days of Leonidas and his Spartan band has the sun shown on a braver company.

The soft rays of the sun, that were thrown back from a thousand sparkling dewdrops on that April morning, were but the precursor of a gathering glory that was to be reflected · upon them in the far off years.   If the external experience of the actors was different, it was by force of mere circumstance; for had each had his own way perhaps he himself would have been foremost, and the first front of the Revolution would have been made by his own company.   This equalizing of honors has been too much overlooked, and in the honest attempt to get at the facts in the interest of exact history, such as the location of dates and the ascription of personal acts to the right parties, there may have sometimes existed questionable rivalry.   But if such is the case it is unfortunate.   Truth requires no invidious comparisons. We may magnify facts, but show no partiality.   Because of incidental circumstances, such as time, distance and population, the parts borne by different towns on April 19th, were from the nature of the case dissimilar.   Be it so, and let that dissimilarity be recognized, but let no favoritism be based upon it.   To Lexington let it be accorded that her town's common land was made sacred by the first blood spilled.   Let Concord claim the first battle ground on which George the Third met with organized resistance.   Admit that Sudbury sent the most militia and minute-men.   Place Acton in the van as she was. And so to all the other towns engaged give the credit that is their due.   Let whatever of especial honor belongs

to them be freely accorded, and then there will remain a
residue of renown which will make each one great.

And so of the individual actors in that never to be for-
gotten conflict, whatever of priority belongs to them as
relates to time, place, or rank, let the honor be recognized.
If Captain Isaac Davis was the first to fall on April 19th,
let the fact be related and recorded, and let no other be
given his place.   If Abner Hosmer was the next to join the
silent procession, which on that memorable morning struck
their tents on earth to spread them "On Fame's eternal
camping ground," let no one deny him the honor.   And if
there followed, a little later, James Hayward and Luther
Blanchard, let it be said of them that they also were faithful unto death, and are numbered among "the few the
immortal names that were not born to die."   Let us inscribe
on granite or bronze their virtues, nor stint them in the
bestowment of a country's gratitude, because death came not
as to the others, on the battlefield, but by slow, lingering
approaches, and through the torture of painful wounds.   To
do this is magnanimous; to do this is just; but to do less
is unjust.

Let us then to each of those, who, on that morning,
which John Hancock said was a glorious one for America,
girded himself for battle, give unstinted praise; remember-
ing, that however much we may extol their valor and admire
their simple virtues, we are in no danger of doing anything
in this direction that will be more than commensurate with
their deserts.   For it was a dark, dark morning that had its
dawning on that April 19th—dark in its uncertainties and
its doubtful issues.   They who entered upon its terrible
experience could not forecast what we see so clearly, that

liberty and light were about to break on a continent. The
future was hidden from their vision. The horizon of their
hope was a narrow one. Their pillar of fire was their faith
in the God of battles. Their cloud was their belief that
His strong arm would prevail.

> "Their feet had trodden peaceful ways ;
>   They loved not strife ; they dreaded pain ;
>   They saw not, what to us is plain,
> That God would make man's wrath his praise.
>
> No seers were they, but simple men ;
>   Its vast results the future hid ;
>   The meaning of the work they did
> Was strange and dark and doubtful then.
>
> They went where duty seemed to call ;
>   They scarcely asked the reason why
>   They only knew they could but die ;
> And death was not the worst of all."

Whittier.

LUTHER BLANCHARD'S LIFE.

II.

The brothers, Luther and Calvin Blanchard, were born in the town of Boxboro, in that portion of its territory which was formerly a part of Littleton.

The deed of the farm on which they were born was, if not the second, at least one of the earliest recorded deeds from "ye proprietors" in the ancient Nashoba plantation. The territory of the old homestead, whose soil was for generations tilled by the Blanchards, is bounded easterly by the so-called "Powers' farm" and southerly by "Indian land;" which latter consisted of about five hundred acres in the southeast corner of Littleton, and was said to be three hundred poles long. It was in the vicinity, if not a part of the exact spot, where the Christian Indians of the Nashoba mission, who were fostered by Eliot and Gookin, made their wigwams and prayed and sang psalms in the deep forest shade, or in the bright sunny openings of the woodland, and neighbored, it may be, with their kinspeople on the green intervales of the Musketahquid river at what is now Concord.

Their father, Simon, was descended from Thomas, who early settled in Charlestown, Massachusetts, in the part which is now Malden. Luther and Calvin probably inherited a martial spirit from their father, for we find his name given among those brave New Englanders, who fought in the intercolonial war between England and France in the period of 1756–1763, and tradition informs us, that he fell on the plains of Abraham at Quebec, fighting under General Wolf, Sept. 13, 1759; so that young Luther's family, at least on his father's side, presumably, was thoroughly imbued with a martial nature, and hence it is not to be wondered at that a later generation should give evidence of its transmission. Some time before his soldier life commenced, he left his home to learn the mason's trade; and we find him at the age of eighteen with his brother Calvin thus employed, and living with Jonathan Hosmer on the place in Acton before described as the site of the memorial stone. As Jonathan Hosmer had a son who was present at the Concord fight, and as they lived not far from the home of Captain Isaac Davis, the gunsmith, it is easy to suppose that the three boys made frequent visits of an evening to his shop, and talked of the probability of war; and when to meet any emergency a minute company was formed, it was only natural for them to enlist under the leadership of neighbor Davis. Luther Blanchard, being a fife player, probably enlisted as the company's fifer, a position of no small importance in those times, when other wind instruments were rare, and the stirring strains of a fife and kettle drum were the usual music on all military occasions. As minute companies were made up more or less of persons of nonage, and others not liable to militia enrollment, frequent drill meetings were quite essential for affording military instruction, and in the various towns some of these drill meetings were held at evening. Probably, weeks before the hostile outbreak, the youthful fifer was present at the drills, and with his fellow musician, Francis Barker, the drummer, played while Captain Davis manœuvered his men in the little lane and practiced them in the manual of arms; and when the company broke rank and was dismissed, naturally enough Luther, and the other boys of his neighborhood, as they wended their way homeward, would have music by themselves, so that doubtless "The White Cockade" was a familiar air to the dwellers in that vicinity. But that little company was not long to play soldier, and when on the evening of April 18th the alarm came to Acton by a mysterious messenger, who at midnight rode through the villages and the lone hamlets, warning the inmates to "up, and to arm!" Among the first to respond was the minute company, which reported in Captain Davis' dooryard early on the morning of the 19th, and received from the faithful commander the assurance that when a sufficient number of men arrived he would march. About seven o'clock, the requisite number had come, and Davis gave the word to start, after declaring that they had a right to go to Concord on the king's highway and that they would do so at all hazards. No sooner had the order to march been given than Luther Blanchard sent out on the cool crisp air the notes of "The White Cockade," and they were off. Little is related in history of the short, quick journey to Concord North bridge, but it is quite probable that when the little band was away they sped

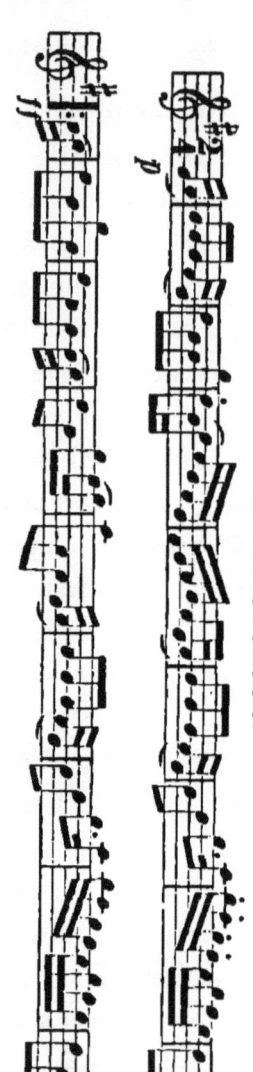

White Cockade.

with flying feet to the time of their own quickened heart throbbings; and that it was only now and then as they slackened their pace at some rising ground that Luther resumed fifing; but when he and his comrades caught a glimpse in the distance of the North bridge, and of the companies from the neighboring towns, we may suppose there was a call for music, and that Luther Blanchard and Drummer Barker did their best; and that the strains coming from afar were to those waiting Middlesex militia men already assembled at Concord, like the sound of the Highlanders' slogan at Lucknow, which long before the musicians were in sight told of the approach of friends. After the meeting of the Provincials near Major Buttrick's, there was a hurried consultation of the officers relative to what should be done and who should do it. While this consultation was going on, smoke arose in the distance indicating that Concord village was burning, and almost simultaneously, a small detachment of Regulars commanded by Lieutenant Gould began taking up the bridge planks to keep the Continentals from going to the rescue. At this juncture of affairs came a crisis, and British power in America began to tremble, for there was one and he the youngest of those commanders, who did not fear to strike down England's arrogance there where it was asserting itself, and declared that "he had not a man who was afraid to follow him." Then came the order to march, and Captain Davis was again on the move, and Luther Blanchard again struck the tune of "The White Cockade," and down they descended the highway by the meadow margin sternly determined upon work, but with orders not to fire till they were fired upon. What a scene was there presented; the sun shining with exceptional brightness, nature dressing herself in gay attire, the birds caroling sweetly in the meadow, and each with Luther as in one grand matineé endeavoring to enliven the eventful hour.   Yes, all was exceptional, the march, the music, the men; but there was to be one thing more to complete the effect, and that was the firing of "The shot heard round the world." Soon it came. As the company drew nearer the river bank, the Regulars, fearing they would be upon them before the bridge could be dismantled, fired a volley.   As there was at first no visible effect produced it was supposed that only blank cartridges had been fired, or that the enemy had aimed their guns into the air. But to make sure that the shots were harmless, Captain Davis asked his company if balls were fired, whereupon Luther Blanchard exclaimed, "Yes, for one has struck me." This was enough for Davis to know, for the invaders had shown themselves murderous; and word was immediately given to fire.   As Davis was raising his gun to take aim, the Regulars fired again and he fell, shot through the heart. Almost simultaneously there fell near him Abner Hosmer, who was shot through the head.   So opened the action of that fateful morning.

As the general causes that contributed to the conflict at Concord are more or less familiar to readers of American history, it is unnecessary for us to consider them in detail, however interesting they might be as incidentally related to the crowning act in the life of Luther Blanchard and his brave compatriots; but it may be appropriate, before following further the fortunes of our hero, to briefly give the outline of some of them.

The conflict at the North bridge was occasioned by

the culmination or result of several events, all of which were incidental to the general plan of Colonel Smith, who had charge of the English forces, to march to Concord, and destroy what military stores were found there and perhaps capture Colonel James Barrett. As at Lexington, it was probably no part of an original design to slay any of the inhabitants nor to destroy private property, unless in furtherance of the general plan. But events conspired to convince the English commander that the Continentals contemplated resistance, and he took precautions to meet it; which precautions precipitated the encounter at the bridge. According to the best information from sources both English and American, the main facts in the case are as follows:

After the massacre at Lexington, which occurred about sunrise, the Regulars proceeded to Concord, not perhaps without some misgivings as to the day's results, since the assembled militia men and the slaughter of some of them was doubtless suggestive of an aroused condition of the country. On the arrival about seven o'clock at Concord village, Colonel Smith and Major Pitcairn took their position in the hillside burying ground, where they could survey operations, disposing of their troops as follows: Captain Mundy Pole of the tenth regiment with about one hundred men was sent to the South bridge; Captain Lawrence Parsons with six companies of infantry, consisting of about three hundred men, was sent northerly, towards the Colonel Barrett neighborhood; the remainder of the force, consisting of four or five hundred men, was retained as a reserve or body guard in Concord village. Of the forces sent northerly, three companies with Captain

Parsons proceeded to the residence of Colonel Barrett to destroy public stores; while three were left, under command of Captain Lawrie, near the North bridge, perhaps with the two-fold purpose of keeping open a way of retreat for Captain Parsons, and of preventing any Provincial soldiers from destroying the bridge. Of the three companies under Captain Lawrie left in the vicinity of the bridge, two straggled off, or scattered about, leaving only one, and that under command of Lieutenant Edward Thornton, to guard the bridge.

In the meantime, the Americans from neighboring towns were assembling at Punkatassett hill, northerly of the river, where were already stationed some of the Concord, Acton, and Lincoln men, who under command of Captain George Minot, had rendezvoused at that place upon the near approach of the Regulars to Concord village. About ten o'clock, while Captain Parsons' men were engaged in mischievous work at Colonel Barrett's, burning gun carriages, the Provincials, having been joined by the Acton minute company, marched from Punkatassett along the highway to Major Buttrick's, which was about forty rods from the North bridge. Here the consultation of officers before referred to took place; the result of which was the forward movement of the Acton minute company, followed by all the others, the firing, the wounding of Luther Blanchard, and the killing of Davis and Hosmer. The fire was returned by the Americans, and several of the English soldiers fell, either wounded or killed.

After this firing, there is little or no evidence of hostilities on either side for more than an hour. Lieutenant Gould and his guard at once betook themselves to the village. Three signal guns were fired by the British at the village to call in the various detachments, all of which soon joined the main body, which about twelve o'clock began its march back to Boston, carrying with them their wounded in vehicles confiscated for the purpose. Meanwhile, the Provincials, who had been reinforced by a minute and militia company from Sudbury, commanded by Captains Haynes and Nixon, hurried across the fields to the easterly of Concord village; and upon their arrival at the Lexington road, awaited the coming of the British regiments, which soon hove in sight. Then commenced that famous wayside warfare, which was kept up with such disastrous results to the English troops until they arrived in Charlestown. The spot where the Acton minute-men stood at the time of the firing is probably a few rods to the rear of the statue of the "Minute-Man." Judge John S. Keyes locates the spot where Davis fell, as at or about the place where at the present time a small bushy apple tree is standing. This is probably correct. That it is no nearer the bridge may perhaps be inferred from the following reasons: 1st. It is hardly to be supposed that the Regulars would allow the Americans to come nearer before firing, if they fired at all. 2d. If the opposing forces had been nearer together, it is probable that the loss would have been greater on both sides. 3d. It has been stated by good authority, that the shot that hit Luther Blanchard was fired when the Americans were within ten or fifteen rods of the bridge. This would place his company on that portion of the causeway over the meadow land, which tradition informs us had stepping stones placed along its edge, to enable foot travelers to pass the road to the bridge at high water. It was upon one of these stepping stones that Captain Davis is said to have fallen, when, after being struck by the bullet, he leaped into the air and fell first upon a stone and then upon the moist ground.   Although nearly, if not all traces of the old causeway to the bridge have disappeared, it is gratifying that the adjacent meadow beyond the " Minute-Man " enclosure, and the site of the old roadway, probably, remain nearly as they did of old, and that the hand of man in its attempt at art has not yet by its would be embellishment quite obliterated the spot where Luther Blanchard was hit, and Captain Davis and Private Hosmer fell.   Still the frosts and the evening damps creep over the moist intervale ; still the blackbird and bobolink sing there ; still the floods rise and fall, and spring as laughingly trips over the turf as when that strange, strange scene was enacted long ago.

But sufficient has been given of the history of the day and its events in their more general features, and we will now resume our narrative in its closer relations to the subject of our sketch.

After Luther Blanchard was hit by the musket ball at the bridge, he went to the house of Humphry Barrett to have the wound bandaged, and later with the other Provincials pursued the ministerial troops to Boston, fifing along the way.   Tradition states, that after arriving at Cambridge, he went into a hospital in one of the Harvard College buildings and shortly after died there from the effect of this wound.   But we think that tradition, which sometimes may claim too much, does not in this case claim enough ; for the evidence of record is that Luther Blanchard like many others, who so ardently beat back the British battalion from Concord, enlisted for the siege of

Boston which immediately followed, and that he was present at the Battle of Bunker Hill, June 17th, and died the September following. If this is the case, then a new leaf is added to the laurels that are already so thickly entwined about the name and fame of Luther Blanchard. And so consequential is it to his memory, that a brief outline of the evidence is given for the reader's consideration.

1st. On the 24th or 25th of April, about twenty-two of the Acton soldiers enlisted for the siege of Boston, and were placed with some Lincoln soldiers in a company that was commanded by Captain William Smith of Lincoln, and assigned to the regiment of Colonel John Nixon.

2d. Among the men in Captain Smith's company accredited to Acton, is the name of Luther Blanchard.

3d. We have not seen it claimed that there were two by this name from the town of Acton.

4th. Captain Smith returned to the Provincial authorities the name of Luther Blanchard on his pay-roll.

5th. There is a tradition, that while Calvin Blanchard was absent in the expedition that went to Canada through the wilds of Maine, under the command of General Benedict Arnold, his brother died and was buried.

6th. The expedition of Arnold set forth from Cambridge in September 1775, and was absent several months.

7th. The wound received at the Concord North bridge was apparently at the time not considered a severe one; judging from the fact that it was not known that anyone was hit, until it was reported by Luther Blanchard in reply to the inquiry of Captain Davis, whether the British fired bullets, and also from the fact that he could follow the Regulars to Charlestown.

8th.   Luther Blanchard's name is on a receipt dated July 7, 1775.   This was for bounty due on account of services in Captain Smith's company, Colonel John Nixon's regiment.   This signature is supposed to be his autograph. Coat Rolls.   Eight months' service.   State Archives, vol. 35, page 62.

9th.   The name of Luther Blanchard, with rank of Corporal, is on the muster roll of Captain Smith's company, Colonel Nixon's regiment, August 1, 1775.   Date of enlistment April 24, 1775.   Time of service, three months, fifteen days.   Belonged in Acton.   This was an order for advanced pay, dated Cambridge, July 7, 1775.

10th.   Luther Blanchard, with rank of Corporal, is on company return of Captain Smith's company, Colonel Nixon's regiment.   Dated Sept. 30, 1775.   Belonged to Acton.   Reported dead.   Coat Rolls.   Eight months' service.   State Archives, vol. 56, page 28.

Such are some of the reasons for belief, that the youthful fifer was on the first two battlefields of the Revolutionary War, and that while enlisted for the siege of Boston, and after the Battle of Bunker Hill, he died at the Harvard College hospital.

After the stirring scenes of April 19th, the college buildings were thrown open to be used as barracks for the soldiers, and continued so to be used until after the evacuation of Boston, March 17, 1776, when the American army went to New York.   As it was used for a barrack, it might if needed, be used as a hospital.

It was quite natural, that the Acton minute-men should enlist for the seige of Boston in a company that belonged to the regiment of Colonel John Nixon, for Colonel Nixon was a citizen of the neighboring town of Sudbury, and one of the Sudbury companies was also of his regiment. During the summer that followed the Concord fight, this regiment was quartered at Winter Hill, now in the city of Somerville.

Before passing, it may be proper to state, that if Luther Blanchard did, as is indicated, share in the battle of June 17, he was in a regiment, and at a place first in importance and peril of any in that terrible conflict, which, a recent English author has stated, was, in proportion to its duration and the number engaged, one of the fiercest and most sanguinary of history.

The regiment of Colonel John Nixon was between the redoubt on the hill summit and the river Mystic, which was held by Colonel Stark of the New Hampshire militia, and was only protected by a few fence rails and a little newly mown hay; yet, it was defended in a manner that was most masterly, and the Regiment was one of the last to leave the field.

And now as we have been tracing the short soldier career of Luther Blanchard, let us pause and reflect upon the service that he rendered to his country as a fifer. The simple music of the fife and snare drum was, in those times, considered very consequential on all military occasions, and to begin a march or engage in battle without them would, doubtless, have been thought disadvantageous.

"The pomp and panoply of glorious war" had not then become obsolete; the gilt epaulet and the plumed military hat for the officers, and martial music were still in use. The fifer and drummer were then very essential, and might turn the scale in a crisis. Their place was near the head of the column, and it was here that we find our youthful hero in those moments that tried men's souls. Young Luther Blanchard is described as at the head of the column when it marched down the little cottage lane from the Davis door-yard, and we first hear of him as sending forth strains on that eventful spring morning.

If ever that little company needed the stimulus that might come from his fife it was at the start. For aught Davis and his comrades knew, they were going to Concord alone. Communications had not come to them as to what others were on the way. They were leaving father and mother, children and home, to face a merciless enemy, who might kill or capture as best suited them. Naturally, then, a shadow might have crept through that early sunlight, and the undertone of their deep apprehensions might have been louder than the sweet carol of the robin in the wayside apple trees. But there was one to cheer up their spirits, however much they might droop ; and, as young Luther stepped at the head of the little brave band, and Francis Barker took his place beside him, the sharp, piercing notes of that fife, now rising and falling, now rolling and mingling with the rat-a-tat-tat and the whiz and the whirr of the kettle-drum, doubtless drove back dismal forebodings and lightened each heavy footstep, so that when the great road was reached every man was in a mood for double-quick. As the Acton minute-men came into Concord territory, the music of their bold fifer was again brought into practical requisition, when they met, a short distance from the North bridge, on the way to Major Buttrick's, militia and minute-men from the towns of Bedford, Chelmsford, Carlisle, Littleton, Westford, Billerica, and Stow. These men had been rendezvoused in the neighborhood of

THE START OF THE ACTON MINUTE COMPANY, APRIL 19th, 1775.

Colonel James Barrett, about two miles from Concord meeting-house, where three companies of British Regulars, under command of Captain Lawrence Parsons, were destroying military stores and gun-carriages. This meeting is graphically related by Frederic Hudson in *Harper's Magazine*, May, 1875 : " On their arrival at the cross-roads, they were met by the Acton minute-men, Captain Isaac Davis. This company, about forty in number, came by the strawberry hill road till they reached the rear of Colonel Barrett's residence. They halted there for a short time, to observe the movements of the detachment of the enemy searching the house. Then, partly by a cross-road, and partly over the fields north of Barrett's mills, they marched by a quick step, the fife and drum playing ' The White Cockade,' in nearly a straight course to the Widow Brown's tavern. Thence they took the north road to the high land, where they met Major Buttrick and his men."

Again, when at Major Buttrick's, by the North bridge, after careful consultation, the continental officers decided that the bridge should be saved, and that if Concord village were burning they should rescue it. Then we read that as the Acton minute-men faced from the right, Luther Blanchard and John Buttrick, the young fifers, playing " The White Cockade," advanced to the scene of action, and placed themselves in an exposed position in the rough, narrow highway. Could the music of that moment have been other than an inspiration to those minute-men to live by or to die by ? Whether it were so or not the yeoman soldiery rushed on to the uncertain conflict, nor did the fray long cease, till there was left no foeman beyond the protection of the English warships at Boston. But not only in the

Davis dooryard and at the North bridge, was there occasion for inspiring the Provincial soldiers by the stirring strains of Blanchard's fife and Barker's drum, but here and there along the line of the British retreat were sharp skirmishes, when the Regulars, too hard pressed by their persistent pursuers, would face about and try to check them by momentary conflict.   Easily may we suppose, that at such times, the bold musicians would improve the opportunity as they stood with their leaders on the very firing line, and threw out into the smoke-begrimmed atmosphere the few simple tunes that they knew.   And so, along the entire course from Concord, as the English hosts made their wild rush in retreat, fighting, faltering, falling, above the loud shouts of the hastening multitude, mingling with the dim and the dust, the cheers of the living and the groans of the dying, might the strains of the fifer be heard; and when at Lexington, Earl Percy with his two field pieces came up to reinforce the returning Regulars, and afforded a little respite to the combatants on both sides, we may suppose again that there was a "band concert" and that Luther Blanchard, John Buttrick, and Caleb Brown, fifer of the Sudbury minute-men, and other fifers, who were doubtless there, played together the tune of "The White Cockade," in a way that made the combatants almost forget their weariness, and grow impatient to renew the strife.   The fifers were among the first to be summoned and among the first to respond.   At Lexington, Jonathan Harrington, the fifer of the militia company there, was aroused by his patriotic mother about one o'clock in the morning, as she shouted, "Jonathan, you must get up!   The Regulars are coming, something must be done!" At Concord, Major John Buttrick, when the alarm reached him, called his son John, a boy only sixteen years of age, and a fifer in Captain Brown's minute company, exclaiming as he did so, "John, the bells are a ringing. Jump up! Load your pistols, take your fife, we'll start immediately for the village." The father and the mother did not hesitate to call the son. War's rude alarm had reached them. To the sound of the tocsin the clan was giving ready response, and the piper should not be away. But those drum beats are over, and the fifer and his fife are silent. The grand procession of that day so ill-starred to Great Britain, and all glorious to America, has ended its march. The years, the fast gathering years have brought havoc alike to either combatants. Nature still holds to her courses, but man and his works have changed. The quiet cattle graze in the fields and pasture places, from which the Provincials once poured their destructive fire. The same river moves purling along on its gentle way, but it flows no longer beneath its ancient archway.

"The foe long since in silence slept ;
 Alike the conqueror silent sleeps ;
And Time the ruined bridge has swept
 Down the dark stream which seaward creeps."

As we have now described the start, the arrival at the North bridge, and the service rendered by the youthful fifer, our narrative might not be considered complete without a description of the route taken by Luther Blanchard's company, and a tracing of that memorable march. This

object we can best accomplish, perhaps, by quoting from
the sketch of Acton history, written by Rev. James Fletcher,
and published in the Middlesex County History, 1890, Vol.
II., page 255 : "It was a bright, genial morning.   The sun
was up at a good cheery height of an hour and a half.   The
birds were chanting the very best songs of the opening
spring.   The men were drawn up in line.   The captain at
last gave the word "march."   Luther Blanchard, the fifer,
and Francis Barker, the drummer, struck at once the stirring notes of the 'White Cockade,' and forward they moved
with a quick, brave step.   They soon reached the homestead of Parson Swift.   They could not wait for the greet-
ings or the partings of the good man, but on they pressed,
with their faces set for Mother Concord.   They moved
along over the old and only road leading from the present
site of Deacon W. W. Davis' crossing in a straight line
through to the meeting-house on the 'knoll.'   The road
struck the other road just below Dr. Cowdry's barn, where
now stands Deacon John Fletcher's barn, just relocated by
Moses Taylor, Esq.   The old road-bed was found when recently digging the cellar for the barn.

"They could not stop for the silent benedictions of the
old church, but the prayers and blessings of the pastor they
could hear, and marched all the faster for the memory.   The
handkerchiefs waving from the Brooks tavern doors and
windows helped the thrill of the hour.   Down the hills
they moved by the present site of Mr. McCarthy, up the
ascent to the right, over the heights on the road path, now
closed, but still a favorite walk down the hill, across the
Revolutionary bridge, west of Horace Hosmer's present
site, the road leading by the spot where the elms south of

his house now stand. Up the hill they hasten and turn to
the right, going by Mr. Hammond Taylor's present residence, the old Brabrook homestead, on the south side,
which was then the front side, the road on the north being
a comparatively new opening; there they left the main
road, struck through the woods, taking a bee line to their
destined point. After passing the woods, the march is by
the Nathan Brooks place, now owned and occupied by Mr.
H. F. Davis. The passage then was by the nearest way
to Barrett's Mills, as then called, not far from the North
bridge."

After arriving in the vicinity of Barrett's Mills, they
marched partly by a cross-road, and partly over a field, as
has already been stated, in a nearly direct line to the
Widow Brown's tavern, and from thence they took the
high land, where they met Major Buttrick and his men,
as before described.

While on the march, they went in files of two abreast.
When they arrived at Widow Brown's tavern, they are described as going rapidly. Charles Handley stated in a deposition, that, at the time of the Concord fight, he lived at
the tavern kept by the Widow Brown, nearly a mile north-
west of the North bridge, and saw Captain Davis' company
as they came from Acton. "I first saw them coming
through the fields north of Barrett's Mills, and they kept
the fields till they came to the road at Mrs. Brown's tavern.
They then took the north road leading to the bridge. They
marched fast to the music of a fife and drum. I remember
the tune, but am not quite sure of its name. I think it
was called 'The White Cockade.'"

In the same double file they marched on to the scene

of action; for after the halt and the hurried consultation of
officers, before described, and the plan to immediately
move forward to the bridge, Captain Davis drew his
sword and ordered his men to advance six paces. He then
faced them to the right, and then to the step of his favorite
tune, he led his command towards the foe.

With regard to their further course and what transpired, the historian Bancroft says:

"The calm features of Isaac Davis became changed.
The town schoolmaster could never afterwards find words
strong enough to express how his face reddened at the
word of command; * * * they went down the hillside,
entered the by-road, came to its angle with the main road,
and then turned into the causeway that led straight to the
bridge."

What next occurred has already been related; firing
followed. Luther Blanchard was hit and Davis and Hosmer fell. Of this sad sequal of that eventful march of
about a half dozen miles, the historian last quoted says:

"Three hours before, Davis had bid his wife and children farewell; that afternoon he was carried home and
laid in her bedroom. His countenance was little altered,
and pleasant in death.

"The bodies of three others of his company, who were
slain that day, were brought also to her home, and the
three were followed to the village graveyard by a concourse
of neighbors for miles around."

Before leaving the part of our subject that relates to
the encounter, it may be of interest to state a few facts
concerning the bridge at which it took place.

The bridge crossed the Concord River to the northerly

of the village, from whence its name the "North bridge."
It was long since demolished, and only a few fragments,
which are preserved as relics, are in existence. One of
these, which is of considerable size, is in possession of
John S. Keyes, Esq., of Concord, who has placed it in a
conspicuous position in the ell of his dwelling-house, and
near a bullet hole, which was made by one of the retreat-
ing Regulars. As the ancient highway was long since dis-
continued, no bridge stood on the spot for some years.
The old historic structure was a plain one; and doubtless
no poet's license was taken by Emerson when he said:

> "By the rude bridge that arched the flood
> Their flag to April's breeze unfurled."

The fragment of timber at the Keyes house looks old and
weather worn, and as if it were of oak as sturdy as the
hearts of the bold farmers, whose hurrying feet once
pressed it.

About three months after the events of April 19, 1775,
two men, Messrs. Dolittle and Earle, the latter having
some skill or fame as an artist, went to the spot and made
a picture of the bridge and its locality. And although not
perfect in its perspective, yet it is quite probable that the
bridge being simple in its construction looks natural. The
northerly bank of the river being low allowed an overflow
of the water, which in the spring and fall freshets came
nearly up to the causeway. Since the year 1875, when the
centennial celebration called public attention to this locality,
and the setting apart of Patriots' Day, the place has been
on April 19th, as a modern Mecca, to whose shrine devotees
of an antiquary taste, as well as those led thither by patri-

otic feeling, have made their pilgrimage, and left their votive offering of reflection and enthusiasm.   The stream, that ran beneath that memorable archway, flows through towns each one of which contributed its quota to that April conflict.   It has its rise in Westboro and Hopkinton, both of which sent soldiers on the Lexington alarm, and on its borders are Framingham, Sudbury, Lincoln, Bedford, Carlisle, Billerica and Chelmsford, so that this sluggish stream, which the Indians called Musketahquid or Meadow brook, might almost be called the river of the Revolution, on whose banks Freedom had its birthplace and from which a waiting world received benefits ; for as Whittier has said in his verse of the patriots of '75,

> " Of man for man the sacrifice
> Unstained by blood save theirs they gave
> The flowers that blossomed from their grave
> Have sown themselves beneath all skies."

Beside the river, and hard by the bridge on the easterly side, is the grave of the two slain Britains, who fell in the return fire of the minute men ; and who, likewise, were faithful unto death ; for, doubtless, they also thought they died doing their duty.   For years, the low mound was grass grown and gray, and utterly forsaken and lone, fulfilling well the description of the burial of Sir John Moore.

> "And the foe and the stranger shall tread o'er his head,
> And we far away on the billow."

At length, kindly hands planted the sheltering pines, and then the music of their murmurings, and the soft ripple of the river waves made a melody befitting the sepulchre of sovereigns.

THE OLD NORTH BRIDGE, CONCORD, MASS., APRIL 19th, 1775.

BLANCHARD MEMORIAL STONE.

III.

The dedication of the Blanchard Memorial Stone was upon a day set apart by the citizens of Acton for exercises commemorative of the battles of Concord and Lexington, and of the going forth of her citizen soldiery to the opening events of both the Revolutionary and the great Civil War.

It was " Patriots' Day" in every sense of the word, and almost the entire population of the town of Acton, and a large portion of the inhabitants of Middlesex County were observing it as a gala occasion, and signalizing it with appropriate exercises.

Simultaneous with the Acton celebration, the neighboring town of Concord was engaged in memorial services, and never since the one hundreth anniversary of the events of April 19th, 1775, at which President Grant was a distinguished guest of the Commonwealth, have the two historic towns been so astir, or entertained a like number of guests. Besides dedicatory exercises at the Blanchard

Memorial, there were exercises at two other historic places, where similar monumental stones had been erected; one, near the site of the Captain Joseph Robbins farm-house, the other near the site of the Captain Isaac Davis house. Among the conspicuous visitors were Governor Green-halge, Ex-Governor Boutwell, and Colonel William M. Olin, Secretary of State. The main exercises of the day were at the centre of the town, where a large tent was spread, in which several addresses were made.

It was a day long to be remembered by the citizens of Acton, and all interested in the scenes and events of old Middlesex; and the new holiday was appropriately and suc-cessfully entered upon the calendar, as time, that by statu-tory enactment belongs to no one in particular but to everyone in general.

The following is taken from the *Boston Journal* of April 20, 1895:

"The little town of Acton, the birthplace of the fore-most heroes of both the Revolution and the Civil War, was the scene of the greatest celebration of Patriots' Day, the one hundred and twentieth anniversary of the Concord fight.

"It was a gala day for the cluster of pretty villages, men, women and children all leaving their homes to attend the fête. Flags and bunting fluttered to the breeze on every hand, the whole town being dressed in its best for the occasion.

"The day could not have been more perfect. It was as beautiful a morning as ever dawned in the uncertain month of April, and delightful summer zephyrs fanned the cheek, while a kindly sun bathed the patriotic scene in a golden glow of sunshine. Booming cannon and pealing bells aroused the town at sunrise. The celebration was a complete success, the exercises were carried out without a hitch, and all Acton was happy at the result, while the visitors had naught to say but words of unstinted praise.

"The crowd was a big one for so small a town, and the hospitality of the place was taxed to its utmost, yet there was room for all, and everybody was comfortably housed, and food and refreshment was as plentiful as the air.

"With the arrival of the first train at nine o'clock in the morning, when the stirring music of two bands sounded out on the quiet air, the celebration commenced, and it was not until the early hours of this morning, when the last strains of waltz music at the grand ball had ceased, and the last dancers sought their homes, that the one hundred and twentieth anniversary of the Concord fight was over, and Acton rested from her fête.

"At nine o'clock the first formal exercises of the day began, when the Committee of Arrangements, headed by Hon. Luther Conant, President of the day, met at the railroad station to welcome and receive the invited guests and other visitors, who arrived on a special train.

"Profuse and artistic decorations made the main street one line of waving color. The most conspicuous point in the whole town was the seventy-five foot granite monument, which towered heavenward like an obelisk, while strings of streamers and flags were hung on all sides of it. A flagstaff pierced the atmosphere twenty-five feet above the monument, and from this elevated position floated the Stars and Stripes. At sunrise, noon and sunset the bells pealed and the cannon boomed. During the intervals the bands gave concerts on the common, playing patriotic airs appropriate to the occasion."

THE ROBBINS HOUSE MEMORIAL.

The first of the memorial stones dedicated was the one erected near the site of the Captain Joseph Robbins house at East Acton. The following is from the *Boston Journal* of the date before mentioned :

"Conspicuous by the roadside, about half-way from the railroad station to the cemetery, is a big rough boulder with the side facing the highway inscribed :

"'Site of house where first alarm was given in Acton! Morning of 19th April, 1775. Capt. Robbins! Capt. Robbins! The regulars are coming!'

"Hardly a single farm-house can be seen from this historic spot. The graven stone stands on the crest of a small hill, while in all directions extend the rough stone walls which mark the boundaries of the pastures and fields.

"Rev. Franklin Parker Wood of Acton, invoked the divine blessing, and Hon. Luther Conant, President of the Day, introduced as one of the older citizens, whose memory of the patriotic days was still fresh, Mr. Moses Taylor, who read an interesting paper in regard to the history of the spot.

"On the 19th of April, 1775, 120 years ago today," began the speaker, "was seen a company of Continental Militia on a march to Concord from this spot, with an order from a horseman about 3 o'clock in the morning, whose name was never known, going at full speed up to

this house, then occupied by Capt. Joseph Robbins, the
commissioned officer in the town, this house being nearest
to the North Bridge, and struck as if with a heavy club, as
they thought, on the corner of the house, three times, not
dismounting, but crying out at the top of his voice, ' Capt.
Robbins! Capt. Robbins! Up! Up! The regulars are
coming to Concord rendezvous at Old North Bridge.
Quick as possible alarm the citizens of Acton.'

"The exercises closed with the dedication and prayer
by Rev. Edward G. Porter of Dorchester."

The spot where this stone stands is, as has been
stated, an exceptionally secluded one. To the westerly is
that little city of the dead, the town's common burying
ground, which is now the dwelling place of all that is
mortal of many who marched on that memorable occasion
from that now forsaken door yard, in response to the midnight rider, who rapped at the Robbins house, while but
a few miles to the easterly is the place of the encounter at
the North bridge; to the northerly and southerly are quiet
woods and pleasant pasture lands. Surely could the dead
rise from their honored sepulchres, we might expect if ever,
they would do it here; and that the precincts of that lone
homestead site would again be thickly peopled by the
sturdy yeomanry, as they met and reported as of yore to
their commander, "All present or accounted for."   But

"No sound can awake them to glory again;"

and the curious visitor can sit undisturbed, while busy
fancy plays with the past, and pushing back the curtain of
intermediate years, takes a peep at Captain Joseph Robbins
as he buckles about him his sword belt as a badge of com-

mand, but perhaps takes down his fire-lock for service. Perhaps before he starts out he goes to a broad corner beaufet and snatches a morsel for his scant morning meal, or thrusts the "logger" on the backlog to prepare a bowl of warm drink of some sort. But the beaufet has crumbled and the "logger iron" long since grew cold, and all that remains of what stood there that morning is in melancholy ruin; and the winds, the sunbeams, the birds and bees have the place all to themselves, save when the passing traveler steps reverently to read and reflect upon the inscription on this new votive stone.

From the site of the Robbins house, the company passed to Woodlawn cemetery, where exercises were held. This burial place contains the graves of many revolutionary soldiers, which were designated by small flags. One incident of the services at this place was the reading by Rev. F. P. Wood from a bible formerly used by Rev. John Swift, Acton's first pastor.

CALVIN AND LUTHER BLANCHARD MEMORIAL.

From the cemetery, the company proceeded to the site of the Hosmer house, near which is the Blanchard memorial stone.

The exercises here consisted mainly of an address by Rev. W. R. Buxton, pastor of the Congregational church, South Acton, and the reading of an historic paper by Hon. Luther Conant.

ADDRESS.

"Fellow-Citizens from Acton and visiting friends from elsewhere :—

We are met together this morning to dedicate this

monument to the memory of two of the men who fought at Concord.

I ask you to turn for a moment from the livelier side of this day's celebration, and picture, in imagination, the appearance which Acton wore just one hundred and twenty years ago to-day. There then lived in this historic town people whose hearts were filled with the love of liberty, and who stood in dread anxiety concerning the future of their Massachusetts Colony. The order to crush any incipient uprising had been given to the King's officers, and those officers were already not far from this vicinity to carry out the orders which they had received. The inevitable had long been expected. The patriots of this portion of Middlesex had slowly but surely been educating fathers, mothers and children to a real understanding of the issues involved and the trend which events were rapidly taking; and, so it was that when, on April 19th, 1775, the first blow was struck by the enemy, the whole of Acton, Concord, and the surrounding settlements, rose up as one man to repel the invader. Patriotism was not, on that memorable morning, confined to any special place or family in this vicinity. In every true Acton home there was a determination to resist the aggressive impertinence of the royalty across the sea.

Well, now, one hundred and twenty eventful years have gone by since the Concord fight. During this time great changes have taken place. Gettysburg and Appomattox have been added to Concord and Bunker Hill; tens of thousands of brave officers and soldiers have followed the path to glory, which Captain Davis and his minute-men traveled; and, yet, our reverence and admiration for the patriots of 1775 do but increase with the lapse of time. We still instinctively turn. at every approach of April 19th, and think of these special places sacred in the annals of liberty, and of these particular men of Acton and Concord who took part in that earliest struggle for independence.   Whatever changes have taken place in our great country, whatever modification our ideas of liberty and government have undergone since that early day, wheresoever the descendants and successors of fathers of the Revolution meet this day to celebrate their deeds and heroisms, the fact is, we still refer back to the *men* who did that work as individuals, and, when the cause of the Revolution is mentioned, however freely outsiders may indulge in theories and abstractions, the people who now dwell in these peaceful towns, the descendants of the men who fought in that glorious war, well understand that the struggle for liberty and right then and always means personal sacrifice, personal devotion, and when you mention the Concord fight, these people know full well that there was a fight—that it was no mock battle between liberty as an abstraction and tyranny as an abstraction, that, indeed, it was a fight to the death between liberty and tyranny incarnate in persons, and that that struggle meant the total surrender of personal ambition and interests and lives.

Now I want to tell you that this is just as it always must be with people having sound views and sane sentiments as to the nature of this ceaseless struggle for better things.   For what is the meaning of the honor which our country is accustomed to pay to the memory of its brave heroes and martyrs ?   Certain it is that the universal instincts of people are deeply rooted in the everlasting depths of good sense and certain it is that when the citizens of Acton this morning instinctively turn to do honor to the memory of these special men for their patriotic services, there is a feeling that the glory of the cause which those men represented at the old North bridge was not to be found in any abstract principle or hollow theory, that indeed the principles and rights for which these men fought appear to us glorious only because those principles and rights were realized and given expression in true hearts, patriotic souls, individual men, and self-sacrificing lives. Principle or right when not expressed in personal struggle is of no more consequence to the world than is the latent electricity that is stored in the atmosphere and elements.

Calvin and Luther Blanchard went to the Concord fight on that memorable morning, not in defense of any abstract principle of which they felt nothing. Those men's hearts and lives were the human batteries in which the divine electricity of liberty was generated and utilized. I have no doubt but that as they went to Concord with Captain Davis and their fellow patriots they feelingly called to mind the tragic end which their father met at Quebec when fighting against the French in 1759. Doubtless they felt that a similar fate might await them that day. It is this expression of right and principle in personal sacrifice and courage that impels us to honor them as individual men. Wherever a minute-man stood, there liberty dared to express itself clearly and fearlessly, and there no disloyalty to principle could come. The men of Acton and Concord had flesh and blood as we have, and let us rejoice that with that flesh and blood there was a considerable alloy of principle and love of right to cast a halo of glory about their deeds.

With what spirit, then, shall we dedicate this plain monument to the memory of these two Acton patriots of '75 ? Ought we not to dedicate it in the same spirit with which the services of the men we honor were rendered at the old bridge ? Can there be any real dedication without the feeling that these men were true to country and gave their lives into the hands of God to be used at that special time as the living expression and defense of liberty, so, to make this ceremony real and free from hypocrisy, we also are to present our own individual lives to God to be used by Him as the vehicles for bringing liberty and happiness to our countrymen and ourselves ? In other places in this town our fellow-citizens will, this morning, pay a similar tribute to the memory of other patriots of the Revolution ; but our special duty is concerned with this special place, and with the memory of these particular men. We dedicate this monument in honor of these two men who were faithful at their particular posts of duty ; and we will ask the Supreme Author of liberty that, as the devotion of these two patriots involved the veritable laying down of life in defence of right, real as the large boulder that now stands before us, so may you and I put into our work the same reality that was in their work, and because they were *men, living beings*, with right and truth incarnate in heroic lives, let this monument stand here and tell to all passers by and coming generations, that the defence of the nation's liberties and institutions is secure only when, in obedience to the law of the divine incarnation, the rights and liberties of the people are given an anchorage in the very hearts and lives of individual men and women."

HISTORIC PAPER.

"With those who interest themselves in the research of genealogy for the purpose of discovering a distinguished pedigree to boast of, or a coat of arms to emblazon their heraldry, we have little sympathy.

"But when we find a man who is willing to give time and money to ascertain if one of his kindred or ancestors suffered or perished in some great cause, and whose memory and acts are passing into oblivion, because historians have not done justice to his services, at once the act commands our admiration and respect, and we bow to him as to a public benefactor.

"From this farm went Calvin and Luther Blanchard to Concord fight and Bunker Hill, sons of Simon Blanchard, who was killed at the Battle of Quebec, 1759. These young men were learning the mason's trade, and could not claim the town of Acton as their birthplace, having been born in what is now the town of Boxboro.

"The story of Luther Blanchard, fifer, and Francis Barker, drummer, taking their places at the head of the line, striking up the tune of 'The White Cockade,' in my early childhood, strongly appealed to my imagination, and I never visit the historic ground without their almost visably appearing before me. Luther was the first man hit by a British ball at the Old North bridge and went to the house of Humphrey Barrett to have his wound bandaged.

"On the 24th of April, five days after the Concord fight, Luther Blanchard, together with fifteen other members of Captain Davis' company, enlisted in Captain William Smith's company of Lincoln, Colonel John Nixon's

Regiment, and was at the Battle of Bunker Hill. After the lapse of one hundred and twenty years, through the generosity of one of his kindred, his grandnephew, Mr. Luke Blanchard of Acton, a noble memorial has been erected to his memory.

"This place has now become one of Acton's shrines, for on this farm dwelt Abner Hosmer, who was killed with Captain Davis at the old North Bridge.

"The other brother, Calvin, was a member of the Westford company in Colonel William Prescott's Regiment. He was a man of great determination and physical strength, both of which qualities came into great prominence on such a day as the Battle of Bunker Hill. He afterward enlisted in the army that under Arnold made an attempt to capture Quebec in the latter part of 1775, where his father was killed sixteen years before."

Rev. E. I. Lindh, pastor of the Baptist Church of West Acton, closed the exercises with the dedicatory prayer.

As in other parts of this publication we have spoken of this memorial stone, it is unnecessary for us to observe further about it here, other than to state that the stone dedicated marks the locality of a homestead from which two notable persons on April 19th, 1775, went forth, and from which, perhaps, as many went as from any one house to the Concord fight. For, it was not only the home of Luther Blanchard, the fifer, and Calvin, his brother, but of Abner Hosmer also, who was one of the first to be slain at the bridge. The old house was demolished many years ago, and stood on the very spot now occupied by the dwelling-house of Herman A. Gould. It was a large house, up-

THE JONATHAN HOSMER HOUSE, APRIL 19th, 1775.

right in front, with a lean-to roof on the back. It had two rooms in front, with an entry between. A large chimney was midway of the house. The back chambers were low and unfinished.

Deacon Jonathan Hosmer, the father of Abner, was the first settler on the farm. Nathan Davis Hosmer, grand-son of Deacon Jonathan, built the dwelling-house now standing, and was the last Hosmer to own the farm.

But as the house and the boys who went from it, so the worthy owner of the house at that time, Deacon Hosmer, should have due recognition for the part he performed in the grand play. The contribution of so many members of his household to attend the frequent drill meetings, that preceded April 19th, required considerable time, and may have caused much interruption. The meetings were held about twice a week, from November, 1774, to April, 1775, and according to the deposition of Solomon Smith, a member of Davis' Minute Company, the price paid by the town of Acton for this service was at the rate of eight pence per half day.

Three young minute-men, making their home in the farm-house, would be almost a small army of itself, and the little squad could "stack arms" about the broad fire-place, and bivouac in miniature beside it, as Luther tuned up with his fife, and the venerable deacon, who was doubtless an old militiaman, instructed the boys in those rudiments of war, which they were already learning in Isaac Davis' door-yard.

That the heart of this patriotic householder was in the work, even if he could not go himself, is evident from the fact, that during the day of the Concord fight he went out

to ascertain, if possible, some tidings of the soldiers, and
that on his return he groaned, as he passed the window to
go into the front door.   Jonathan Hosmer was, at the time
of the events here related, a deacon in the Acton Congregational church, and was sixty-five years old.   He died in
1775, and it may be that his demise was hastened by the
death of his son.

On the morning of the 19th, the old house was doubtless made very lively by hearing of the alarm.   In a
moment, probably, candles gleamed from several windows,
and, perhaps, no sooner did Luther, Calvin, and Abner
hasten down stairs and through the entry-way than they
were met by an anxious mother, who was already
hurrying to arouse them; and, as they hurried into the
kitchen, we may suppose they found there the deacon,
poking from the back log the ashes with which he had
banked it the night before, or casting upon the already
glowing coals some light brush-wood to hasten the early
breakfast.   Had the boys not waited for breakfast, however, they would not have gone to the battle-field hungry,
for history informs us that for those who arrived at the
Davis cottage without having breakfasted, Mrs. Davis prepared a morning meal, the men meanwhile employing
themselves in making cartridges.

But while this spot is suggestive of fervor and patriotic
endeavor, it is also suggestive of sadness.   Two, who went
from this home that morning, never came back ; and of all
who then went forth, it may be said, they went to die or to
suffer.   Abner was brought back in the embrace of death,
a few hours after he hopefully left his father's door-yard
trailing or shouldering his gun, and his prostrate form was

borne up the little lane to the door of the Davis cottage, and laid by the form of his faithful leader to await the coming of another, who was soon to join that silent company; for the funeral of Davis, Hosmer, and James Hayward was held in a single service by Rev. John Swift at Captain Davis' late home. Luther was not there to play over the remains "Saul's March," nor to take a last lingering look upon the faces of comrades whom he doubtless loved, and with whom he had dared so much; but with wound irritated by his long pursuit of the British, he rested in barrack or hospital in the college building in Cambridge, only to go later to conflict, and afterward to be borne back, slowly and sadly by relatives or comrades, past the scenes of a few months previous, to find a grave among his ancestors in the wayside burial place at Littleton.

The cemetery in which his dust reposes is situated near Littleton Common, and has an area of an acre or two, scattered over which is a growth of tall pines, whose gentle murmuring is not inharmonious with the associations of the place. It is in some respects a typical New England burying ground; and the irregular position of many of the head stones is evidence of the lapse of long years since the hand of friendship erected them. The older stones bear date as far back as the first half of the eighteenth century, which is indicative of its having been set apart for its present purpose about that time. No record is known to exist as to by whom or of whom this consecrated ground was procured. It may have been given by "ye proprietors" to whomsoever would occupy it; knowing full well that no arrant trespasser would lay hold of any of that scant acreage till he was obliged to; and then, only to hold it in mortmain. The markers are mostly slate-stones, and in many instances are not only leaning and sunken, but the quaint epitaphs have become mossgrown and weatherworn.

In the Blanchard lot, which is in the easterly portion, and near the front entrance, are several stones of this character, upon which are inscriptions as follows:

"In memory of Mrs. Abigail, wife of Mr. Calvin Blanchard, who died June 12, 1836, Æt 79."

"Sacred To the memory of Mr. Calvin Blanchard, who died Jan^r 2^d 1800.   Aged 46.
"The sweet remembrance of the just,
Shall flourish when they sleep in dust."

"Here lies buried ye Body of John Blanchard, Son of Mr Thomas & Mr^s Sarah Blanchard who Dec^d Octo^{br} 10th A. D. 1745 Age 26 years 10M & 7D."

No stone was erected to designate the grave of Luther at the time of his burial; for, as he died leaving neither wife nor children, his grave shared the fate of many another at that time, and was left unmarked.

The Revolutionary age was an age of the bearing of heavy burdens, and it was no lack of affection that allowed the bodies of the beloved dead to repose without a stone to bear them record.   The stone that bears the name of Calvin, marks the grave of Luther's brother, who went with him to the North bridge, and was afterward killed by the fall of a tree.

After the Concord fight, Calvin continued in the service, and we hear of him at the battle of Bunker Hill, in the regiment of Colonel Prescott, stationed at the redoubt.   He was a man of stout physique, and it is said, that before the battle he assisted in tearing down a barn for material with which to make fortifications, and that he would carry one end of the timber when it required two men to carry the other. As has been stated, Calvin was in the Canada campaign with General Arnold in the fall of 1775, and, while absent, Luther, according to tradition, was borne to his last, long home in Littleton. But while widely separated for a time in life, their mortal remains were not long separate when life had fled; for, in 1800, Calvin was carried to the same little burial place, and buried where now the pine branches droop or sway with the pleasant breezes, and the wild flowers creep in the spring-time to decorate the turf.

> "So sleep the brave who sink to rest
> With all their country's wishes blest."

THE DAVIS MEMORIAL STONE.

Immediately following the Blanchard dedicatory services, were those held near the site of the Isaac Davis home. This spot is about one mile westerly of Acton Centre, at the premises of Charles Wheeler. Upon it has been placed a hewn stone, on the side of which, facing the highway, is the following inscription:

> "THIS FARM WAS THE HOME OF
> CAPTAIN ISAAC DAVIS,
> WHO WAS KILLED IN BATTLE BY THE BRITISH
> AT THE OLD NORTH BRIDGE IN CONCORD,
> APRIL 19, 1775."

An address was made here by the Rev. George F. Clark of West Acton, a part of which is as follows:

"The story of Captain Isaac Davis and his brave associates has been frequently told. But it never grows old, and will not grow old, so long as the love of liberty shall animate the hearts of our citizens. It needs to be retold to coming generations, until throughout the entire world the inalienable rights of men of every race and clime shall be guaranteed. It needs to be rehearsed until 'man's inhumanity to man' shall no longer 'make countless thousands mourn,' and, instead, the ties of universal brotherhood are everywhere acknowledged.

"Learning of the approach of the enemy, Captain Davis quickly prepared to lead his company to the post of danger. His widow affirmed that her husband 'said but little that morning. He seemed serious and thoughtful, but never seemed to hesitate as to the course of his duty.' The hasty preparations for departure being completed, the march began; but, having gone a few rods, a halt was called, and Captain Davis returned to the house and bade his wife good-bye, saying: 'Take good care of the children.' On leaving the town, an hour or more after sunrise, Captain Davis said: 'I have a right to go to Concord on the king's highway, and I intend to go if I have to meet all the British troops in Boston.' This shows the spirit of the man. Arriving at the scene of action, about 9 o'clock, he reported to Adjutant Hosmer that he was ready for duty, and took the position assigned him. Soon the decisive moment came. A movement toward the bridge was made, Captain Davis and his company taking the right and leading the van, exclaiming, as he started: 'I haven't a man that is afraid to go!' No, indeed! For he and his brave compatriots were

> " ' Men, high-minded men,
>   Men who their duties know,
> But know their rights, and, knowing, dared maintain.' "

THE STATUE OF THE MINUTE-MAN.

Erected Near the Spot Where Luther Blanchard was Hit by a British Musket-Ball,
and Capt. Isaac Davis and Abner
Hosmer Fell April 19th, 1775.

THE SIGNIFICANCE

OF

MINUTE-MEN MEMORIAL STONES.

IV.

" Time rolls his ceaseless course.   The race of yore,
   Who danced our infancy upon their knee,
And told our marvelling boyhood legends store,
   Of their strange ventures happ'd by land or sea,
How are they blotted from the things that be ?
   How few, all weak, and withered of their force,
Wait, on the verge of dark eternity,
   Like stranded wrecks, the tide returning hoarse,
     To sweep them from our sight !   Time rolls his ceaseless
       course.

Yet live there still who can remember well,
   How, when a mountain chief his bugle blew,
Both field and forest, dingle, cliff and dell,
   And solitary heath, the signal knew ;
And fast the faithful clan around him drew,
   What time the warning note was keenly wound,
What time aloft their kindred banner flew,
   While clamorous war-pipes yelled the gathering sound,
   And while the Firey Cross glanced, like a meteor round."

Scott.

It is many years since events of greater significance have been celebrated in a Middlesex town, than those now described. Other towns have erected monuments designating battle-fields. Lexington has marked the spot on or near which her citizens fell, at the first fire of the British Regulars; Concord has her minute-man statue by the side of the Old North bridge; and Sudbury has a monument commemorative of a conflict between the Colonial soldiers and the allied Indian forces of Philip of Pokanoket. But when, before the erection of the memorial stones now dedicated, has individual, town, or municipality erected similar souvenirs of the homes of the Middlesex Minute-men? Yet, what could be more fittingly or appropriately commemorated? For, what is more allied by stirring historic association to that formative period of the past, known as the period of '75 and '76, than the dwelling-places of these extemporised soldiers? In those humble homes, which were usually the typical New England farm-house or the quiet cottage of the village artesan, were the hearthstones about which were held those evening and neighborhood talks, where great plans were projected, and where influences had their beginnings which reached into far off years. Greater council chambers there have been in the world's history, where, within palace or castle walls, princes and potentates have assembled to shape the courses of nations, but other councils came after them which undid their work, because they who wrought it would not sacrifice themselves to maintain it; but what was done by the minute-men in the council hall of the old farm kitchen, above whose broad, flaring fire-place was the old king's arm snugly nestled amid squashes and herbs, was carried out at all hazards. To mark the sites of such places is noble, and to search for them among the crumbling brick work of old chimney stacks, where the vagrant cyprus and the straggling bouncing Bess may now and then disclose a bit of half-burnt brand from the last back-log, is better than searching for diamonds.

But let us turn from these homes, and consider briefly who these minute-men were.

The minute-man was created for a military emergency. He was, in this respect, *sui generis*, and his character and history were unique. He might be too old or too young for a militiaman. He relied upon himself for the accomplishment of his object; and he might, perhaps, say, as Roderick Dhu said to FitzJames:

> " Brave Gael, my pass, in danger tried.
> Hangs in my belt, and by my side."

George W. Curtis informed his audience at the Centennial celebration of the Concord fight, that the minute-man of '75 was old Deacon Josiah Haynes of Sudbury, who, at the age of about eighty, went to the Concord fight on horseback; and the historian, Bancroft says: "As the Sudbury company, commanded by the brave Nixon, passed near the South bridge, Josiah Haynes, near eighty years of age, deacon of the Sudbury church, urged an attack on the British stationed there." Perhaps it may be rightly stated that the minute-man of '75 was, for the most part, amenable to no one except to his company officers and his own conscience.

The officers of the minute companies held no commissions from either Congress or Crown. The pay of these soldiers was what a town might vote them. And if, on the return for service rendered on April 19th, 1775, money was granted them by a grateful people, it may have been as a gratuity. Says the historian, Bancroft: "The Congress of Massachusetts adopted a code for its future army, and authorized a committee of safety to form and pay six companies of artillery; yet they refused to take into pay any part of the militia or minute-men." Thus it was that the minute-man was, in a sense, his own man, and as such he had a right to be a foremost man. Because he was a minute-man he was expected to be at the front and form the firing line. Old Deacon Josiah Haynes had a right to urge the Sudbury company to cross the South bridge, on their way to Concord; and it doubtless was from a sense of deference to Colonel James Barrett, who requested that the company rendezvous at the North bridge, that Captain Nixon acceded and went there, and the result was, that Sudbury did not begin the fight. There perhaps need be no wonder then, as to why Captain Isaac Davis, being the youngest of the assembled company commanders, should be the first to face the British Regulars in organized resistance. He had a right to be first, for he was a minute-man; and his company had a right to follow him, for it was a minute company. He said, before starting from Acton, as we have stated, that he had a right to go to Concord by the king's highway, and that he should do so if he met all the British troops in Boston; surely, then, he should not be deterred by waiting for any one to precede him. He knew no toll-gate of stiff etiquette on the county's highway; he recognized no turnpike bar of formality; he would pay no toll except in powder and ball. He had, that morning, fed his men at his own table; they had made cartridges by his fireside, and being a gunsmith, he had, perhaps, furnished some with guns.

If, then, anyone had a right to go to Concord without hindrance, it was this bold leader and his little company. There is little need of controversy, to settle a point, that settles itself, when we consider the circumstances. Davis hurried to reach the place he started for, and beside him was his faithful fifer, who like his leader was probably hit, because at the front. It was minute-man music that Luther Blanchard played that morning, and perhaps the first strains that the English soldiers heard at Concord were from young Luther's fife, and it may be, that the last notes that faded out with the dying day were those of " The White Cockade," which the young Acton musician may have played when near the Charlestown peninsula, thus reminding the Regulars of the remark of the Roxbury school boy, who said, as Earl Percy started out playing "Yankee Doodle," that they might return to the tune of " Chevy Chace."

Such were the Middlesex minute-men; independent, bold to rashness, going from the fireside council of the farm kitchen to the red field of conflict, unflinching, and asking favors of no one. We hear of them among the first to start, and the first to fall. Among the slain along that wayside battle-field, are conspicuous the names of the minute-men, or of those who went with them.

Probably none were more zealous in the great struggle for American independence than was this class of old yeomanry. When the conflict was ended they returned to the peaceful pursuits of their home-life in a spirit as manly and self-reliant as they went forth in the hour of battle; content to till the soil, and to develope their little home industries for such rewards as their frugality and diligence afforded. They formed a republic on the principles which they had fought to secure; and they were as earnest in its maintenance in town meeting and convention, as they were in securing it in the day of conflict.

Though the earthly lives of such men may come to an end, yet there is no death to the influence of their illustrious deeds. It continues with the liberties their efforts and sacrifices have established and maintained. So may it be with each honored name; may it be perpetuated and given a proper place in history.

> " So let it live unfading,
>   The memory of the dead,
>   Long as the pale anemone
>   Springs where their tears were shed,
>   Or raining in the summer's wind,
>   In flakes of burning red,
>   The wild rose sprinkles with its leaves
>   The turf where once they bled ! "
>
> O. W. Holmes.

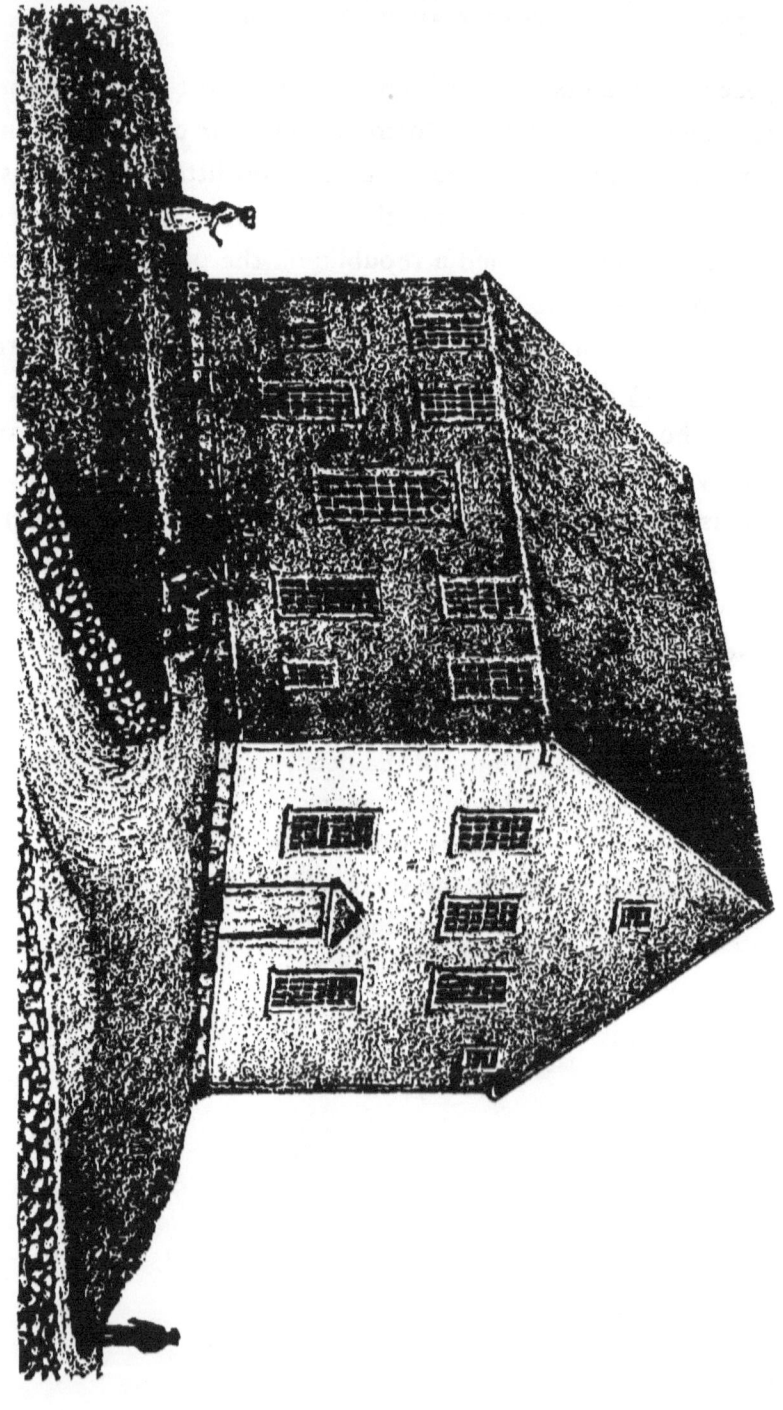

THE FIRST MEETING-HOUSE, ACTON, MASS., ERECTED 1738.

THE MINUTE-MAN

AND THE

NEW ENGLAND MEETING-HOUSE.

V.

The going forth to battle of Calvin and Luther Blanchard, and the class of soldiers whom they represented, was
not a matter of accident or caprice, but was occasioned by
influences which had been at work since the Puritan exodus
from England to the Massachusetts Bay shores, which began about 1630. These influences were intensely religious.
The Puritan's bible, as he read it, was positive in its teach-
ings concerning "A church without a bishop, and a state
without a king;" and although the New England immi-
grant was obliged to build a civic structure under colonial
relations to the British crown, he would only tolerate those
relations so long as they were righteous, and he could do
it consistantly with fealty to God's word. In process of
time he found this impossible, hence a resistance to authority that resulted in organized revolt. Thus was the Revolution the child of pious parentage; and the militia and
minute-men who participated in·it were as much an ethical
and religious creation as the soldier of Cromwell, about a
half century before.

The visible symbol of what constituted the New England minute-man was the New England meeting-house, and the living exponent of the principles it set forth was the minister. Back of every movement of the minute-men was a moral and religious mainspring, tempered fine by what was taught in these homely places of worship, perched bleakly among his own home hills, or nestled snugly in his valleys, or upon his intervales. The cause for which he contended was born in the farm-house parsonage of his minister, who, settled for life, was the oracular authority for what was ecclesiastical and civil, if not militant. The principles of his patriotism were preached on Sundays, and the message was considered heaven-sent. The minister was liberally educated. He was the town's statesman, its umpire in matters of dispute, and the teacher of "higher learning." The meeting-house was the place of town meeting, as well as church meeting, and the church government was, in a broad sense, democratic. From such associations and agencies came forth the militia and minute-men of '75; and thus it may be seen that he was not a special creation, but an evolved product of slow-moving forces.

This estimate of the causes which produced the minute-man magnifies him, and puts him on the high plane of intelligence, where he belongs. There is a correspondence between his high character and the privileges of the last century, although, to a casual observer, these may appear meager and stinted. It was the loftiness of his purposes that gave him his fighting qualities.

The wonder may be sometimes expressed as to why such intelligence went with the provincial soldier to the battle-field, and why it was that there were "bayonets that

could think," at a time when the little red school-house had
been but recently raised on the small, three-sided patch of
the town's common land at the cross-roads, or in some
scant corner of a farmer's close; but the wonder ceases, when
we consider that there were other school-houses; that
the meeting-house helped to educate, and that the church-
going bell was a school bell, and that as surely as its tones
from the little belfry on the common called the yeomanry
to arms in the first gloaming of that April day of conflict,
so surely, on each successive Sabbath in the years that
long preceded, it called the householder's family together
into the hard, pen-like pews, where they learned that "Resistance to tyranny is obedience to God;" that "Taxation,
without representation. is wrong;" and that "All men are
born free and equal." Without a response to the bell in
the first instance there would have been no response in the
last. Without a response in the first instance there would
have been no midnight messenger riding out into the dark-
ness, striking liberty's sparks as he went, and scattering
abroad that alarm that aroused the startled land. No
amount of arithmetic, or grammar, or geography could
make the minute-man of '75; it required years of tutorage in
those educational processes that were inaugurated at the
beginning of each colonial town, when the General Court,
that gave it an incorporated existence, made that existence
conditional upon its maintenance of a gospel ministry.
Hence it was that the minute-man could get along without
the school-house better than without the meeting-house
and the minister; for his minister was his library, his
sermons were his lecture courses, and the Bible his book
of all books.

To show that our position is correct, and to show what the minute-man was in his religious relations, we have only to notice what history says of him in this respect. We are informed by Hon. John S. Keyes, the historian of Concord, that Captain Miles, who commanded a company from that town, stated that "He went to the battle in the same spirit that he went to church;" so it was with other officers of that memorable period, and also of the war period just preceding it.

General John Nixon, who commanded the regiment at Bunker Hill, in which Luther Blanchard fought, was, in his later life, a member of the Sudbury church. Colonel Josiah Brown, who commanded a regiment in one of the Crown Point expeditions, with which regiment, it is supposed, Simon Blanchard was at one time connected, was also prominently connected with this church, and as a token of his regard for it, gave it a piece of land, the proceeds of which were for the supply of the communion elements. Samuel Dakin of Sudbury, who was a captain in Colonel Brown's regiment, in one of the Canada expeditions, thus graphically writes concerning the men of his company, in a letter written to his wife, dated September 25, 1755: "I am in good health, and my company are so obedient to me, and so loving to one another, that it makes my life exceeding comfortable and pleasant. I have never yet heard one thwarting word in my company, but they seem all to have a brotherly care one for another; and have never heard one profane word among them, and their forwardness to attend religious exercises is delightful to me; so that I have many mercies." In a letter of later date, he writes as follows of his company: "They are all well, and I hope I shall be very happy in my company, and they are ever ready to attend prayers, and singing of Psalms, which we have practiced on our journey."

In a memorandum of Captain Dakin's, dated September 27, 1756, he states as follows: "And now, going on an expedition to Crown Point, I have given myself up wholly to God, to be at his disposal in life or death." It is stated that Rev. Samuel Woodward of Weston, when about one hundred men had gathered at the house of Captain Samuel Lamson, on the morning of April 19th., offered prayer, and then, seizing a musket, went with the company in pursuit of the regulars.

We are informed of Rev. John Swift of Acton, that as Captain Davis and his men swept past his house, while Luther Blanchard was playing his fife, he flung after them a pastor's blessing. It was from the house of a deacon in the Acton church, that the three young men, Abner Hosmer, Calvin, and Luther Blanchard went forth; and James Hayward, one of the slain, was the son of another deacon of the same church.

Such was the moral and religious make-up of the militia and minute-men of '75; and such are some of the elements of which their character was constituted. In the world's extended annals, perhaps no man was ever better fitted for his task, and, it may be, results more noble or lofty were never more quickly achieved. Born of such noble purposes, bred in such humble temples, and with a dauntless spirit, made ironclad against cowardice by an unfaltering faith in God, but with such rude accouterments as would invite defeat, he went forth and made a throne tremble, and the right hand of its proud despot loosen its grasp on an oppressed continent.

At the day's dawning of April 19th, the red cross of St. George danced gayly on the folds of a flag whose prestige was a power to them who fought beneath it; at the day's declining that banner had drooped, and many who followed it had fallen never to rise till the great resurrection. They had met the militia and minute-men. They had seen written upon the wall in unmistakable characters, the truth that "bayonets could think," though they who carried them had only been taught of God by their ministers, in their humble meeting-houses among their farms, on their rugged hills. Yes, true it was, that, by a courage born of their character, the militia and minute-men changed the flag of America between sun and sun on April 19th. Sublimely has the poet, Oliver Wendell Holmes, described the contrast in those weary, war-vexed hours, in his poem, "The Battle of Lexington," of which the following is a part:

"Gayly the plume of the horseman was dancing,
  Never to shadow his cold brow again;
Proudly at morning the war steed was prancing:
  Reeking and panting he droops on the rein;
    Pale is the lip of scorn,
    Voiceless the trumpet horn,
Torn is the silken-fringed red cross on high;
    Many a belted breast
    Low on the earth shall rest,
Ere the dark hunters the herd have passed by.

" Snow-gilded crags where the hoarse wind is raving,
   Rocks where the weary floods murmur and wail,
Wilds where the fern by the furrow is waving,
   Reeled with the echoes that rode on the gale ;
      Far as the tempest thrills,
      Over the darkened hills,
Far as the sunshine streams over the plain,
      Roused by the tyrant band,
      Woke all the mighty land,
Girded for battle, from mountain to main.

" Green be the graves where her martyrs are lying ;
   Shroudless and tombless they sunk to their rest—
While o'er their ashes the starry fold flying
   Wraps the proud eagle they roused from her nest :
      Borne on her Northern pine,
      Long o'er the foaming brine
Spread her broad banner to storm and to sun ;
      Heaven keep her ever free,
      Wide as o'er land and sea
Floats the fair emblem her heroes have won.'

THE DESIGN

OF

THE BLANCHARD MEMORIAL STONE.

VI.

He, who preserves one fragment of history that would otherwise be lost, is like one who makes two blades of grass grow where but one grew before, a public benefactor; and he who makes prominent an historic event, that had hitherto been kept too obscure, performs an act which is akin to its preservation.

To render a service of this latter character is one object of the donor of this memorial stone. Luke Blanchard has sought to do justice to one whose well-deserved merit entitles him to a place with his compatriots Davis, Hosmer, and Hayward, whose remains repose within the granite mausoleum at Acton center.

That these four Acton minute-men should be equally honored admits of no doubt. Together they marched down the little country lane that led out into the great world on that calm April morning; and, together hurried to Concord whither it was said by the midnight messenger that the foe was rapidly hastening; together they stood on

Luke Blanchard

the bank of the Concord river, when it alone separated them from some of the best troops of the British throne; together they stood, as their leader offered them an early sacrifice upon their country's altar; and shoulder to shoulder they met the enemy and received his fire.

Yes, as they were not separated in life, so in death they should not be divided. So thought the donor of this memorial stone, and suiting the action to the noble thought he set about erecting that which gives a like prominence to them all. Truly, as Daniel Webster exclaimed at the dedication of Bunker Hill monument, "A duty has been done;" and as in years to come other generations shall make a pilgrimage to this new tribute to departed worth, and shall read the inscription on the one side as it sets forth the name and brief history of Luther Blanchard, the Revolutionary fifer, they will turn with satisfaction and read also the inscription on the other:

"ERECTED IN 1895
BY LUKE BLANCHARD,
GRAND–NEPHEW OF LUTHER."

The work that has been accomplished by the erection of this new memorial is supplemental to the great service done by the State and the Town of Acton in 1851, when it erected the so-called Davis monument to the memory of Captain Isaac Davis, Abner Hosmer, and James Hayward.

Why the name of Luther Blanchard was not inscribed on that memorial may, perhaps, in part be accounted for by the fact that he was not a native of Acton; and if the design was only to record the names of such as were native-born citizens, this explains it.

But we think this is hardly a sufficient reason for such a notable omission, for Acton was the town of Luther Blanchard's adoption; and though born in the adjacent territory, which is now Boxboro, the proximity of the two places was such as might well lead them to hold honors in common. Small difference then should it make as to the relationship of nativity in this instance. But another reason that may be assigned for the unfortunate omission is that young Blanchard died of a wound, and was not killed outright. But so did James Hayward die of a wound. Though he was struck by a musket bullet a short distance from Lexington yet he lingered for some hours. Even if the wound received by Luther Blanchard at the North bridge had not proved fatal, although there is no evidence to show that it was not that wound which, irritated by hard service in the entrenchments at Bunker Hill, caused his death, it is no reason for giving him a second place in history. Tradition says he died of a wound received in battle; and if so, it makes no difference when or where.

He was one of Acton's Revolutionary martyrs, and was laid upon his country's altar; and no monument to the memory of her illustrious children, who fell upon that first memorable morning, can be complete without his name. In erecting, then, this simple memorial, though it be not as imposing in its material proportions as yonder shaft that rises above those other noble slain, yet in its humble symplicity it says as much to the world, and hence, he who erected it is as surely a public benefactor as they who, out of the treasury of a great Commonwealth, have done that which in its material relations is more imposing.

In selecting a suitable stone as a marker of the spot from which his grandfather and grand-uncle went forth to battle, Luke Blanchard had the good taste to take one from the adopted town of those whose deeds it was to commemorate. He selected a natural stone on the soil of Acton, and with painstaking had it suitably inscribed and placed in its present position. In the selection of a memorial stone of such a character, the donor has done an act that is suggestive of the great truth, that it is neither " Storied urn nor animated bust" that make mementoes interesting and valuable, but the character of that which is commemorated. The donor of this monument might, out of his abundant resources, have erected a massive memorial of marble or of bronze, but he has taught us by this simple selection, that a name may make anything great, and that a mere boulder from any of our New England hills, if inscribed with the name of a minute-man of '75, may serve as good a purpose as column or pyramid.

In the erection of a memorial of this kind, more may be accomplished by the donor than we at first suppose. It stands there as a faithful guide-post of freedom, pointing to the path that our fore-fathers trod to obtain it. The way that led from the humble home of Luther Blanchard to the old North bridge was, for all the ardent youth knew, a pathway to the grave, or to exile, or a British prison. The out come of the strife was uncertain, for the issue none could foresee. But the glorious, objective point to those patriotic spirits was as clear and distinct as the sun in the heavens on that bright spring day. What was it to him or his comrades " Though the paths of glory lead but to the grave," they would walk in them, nevertheless, for it was freedom's way they trod, and the priceless boon, for which his father had fallen on the far-off plains of Quebec, was to him as precious as it was to his sire.   And as the traveller stops by this niche in the road by the quiet country-side, he reads on that granite surface, that they who would have rights in-alienable must maintain them at a cost it may be of all that is dearest.   Surely, then, this humble tribute is more than a mere marker of where Luther and Calvin Blanchard once lived, and of the farm from which one went to an early grave, and from which both went forth to glory; it is a guide-board to liberty for the generations to come, and points the way in which we are to preserve our heritage.

Space forbids further suggestions that come from the service done by the donor of the stone.   It speaks for itself, as it stands alone by the wayside.   The tired school boy, as he rests for a moment beside it, the teamster and the toiling laborer, as they pass it in their daily round of duty, the curious traveller and the errandless tramp, all may alike be benefitted as they catch new inspiration, when reminded by this wayside souvenir of the great nobility of man, when it is brought to its highest endeavor in a noble cause.

SIMON BLANCHARD,

Son of Calvin, and Grandson of Simon who was Killed
at Quebec, 1759.

ANCESTRAL ANNALS

OF

CALVIN AND LUTHER BLANCHARD.

VII.

Thomas, the first ancestor of Calvin and Luther Blanchard in America, of whom we have any knowledge, came to this country from near Andover, England, with his son George, born in 1616, on the ship Jonathan, in 1639; and by the best authority obtainable by us, settled in Braintree, Mass. The name of Thomas Blanchard is on the record of that town as early as 1648, and is also found there some years later. At just what date he took his departure for Malden, or what was the cause of his change of abode, we have not ascertained. There is reason, however, for the supposition, that a land purchase from a former pastor of the Braintree church was a chief factor in the case, as history informs us, that Thomas Blanchard, on February 12, 1650–1651, bought a farm of Rev. John Wilson, minister of Braintree, for two hundred pounds. The Wilson-Blanchard farm was in the southerly part of the territory of Malden, near the border of the marsh land. The farm included the entire promontory, which projects out into the marshes near the mouth of the north creek of the Mystic river, and the place was formerly known as "Wilson's Point," and "Blanchard's Point." Its area extended from the Mystic to the small stream or creek, which separates Medford and Malden; and from the north creek easterly of the Craddock grant, according to historian Corey, who states, that, until as late as 1855, traces of the cellar and chimney could be seen upon the highest point of the Wellington farm. After the death of Thomas Blanchard, which occurred in 1654, the house and land was divided between two of his sons, George and Nathaniel; and the latter, in 1657, sold half of his land to his younger brother Samuel, who was at that time building a second house on the estate. In process of time, John Guppy acquired a one-quarter right to the Wilson estate of Nathaniel Blanchard, which was bounded on the north by Nowell's creek, which separates Medford from that part of Malden now Edgeworth. A house on the place subsequently went into the possession of Thomas Shepard.

Some of the Blanchards long lived in the vicinage of the ancestral domains, but by 1795, the last landholder bearing the Blanchard name had left the locality. Years, however, before the paternal estate was wholly abandoned, and conveyed to others, the exodus of one or more representatives of the family, to the territory of what is now Littleton, had taken place; for, as before observed, we hear of Joseph Blanchard, the grandfather of Calvin and Luther, on the ground as early, at least, as 1717–1718. The causes that led Joseph to take up his abode there, were, we believe, two-fold, viz. : The purchase of a large land tract there by Ralph Shepard, a neighbor of his family;

and the marriage of Joseph, his father, son of George Blanchard, to Hannah Shepard, who, we conjecture, was a daughter of Ralph Shepard, formerly an inhabitant of the territory of Charlestown, now Malden. As this conjecture, however, is not based directly on the data of record, but is the result of inference, it is proper to state our reasons for the inference, which are as follows :

1st. We are informed, as a matter of history, that Joseph, son of George Blanchard, born 1654, married Hannah Shepard.

2d. In 1635, Ralph Shepard, with his wife, Thanklord or Thankslord, aged 23, and his daughter Sarah, aged 2, came to America from Stepney Parish, London, England, on the ship Abigail, and after living for a short time in Dedham, Weymouth and Rehoboth, settled in Malden.

3d. The following record is found in the Proceedings of the Littleton Historical Society: "Sarah, born 1633; Abraham, ——; Isaac, born June 20, 1639; Triall, born December 19, 1641, married, 1660, Walter Powers; Thankful, born February 10, 1650; Jacob, born June, 1653; (perhaps) Ralph, who died January 20, 1711 or 12; (perhaps) Daniel ——; Mary, born about 1660–62."

4th. We are informed that the foregoing record is made up, at least in part, from tradition, and is not claimed to be complete.

5th. In that early period of our country, probably, a record of births and deaths was not so carefully kept as in an age which makes the keeping of records compulsory; and, as a matter of fact, as is well known to historians, omissions on public records, of names and dates pertaining to families, are not unusual.

6th.   The sons, Ralph and Daniel, who have, by conjecture, been assigned to the years 1653 and 1660, may
have been born between 1641 and 1650, and in the interim
between 1653 and 1660 one or more children may have had
birth and, if so, they would be of about the age of Joseph
Blanchard, who married Hannah Shepard.

7th.   We have found, upon examination of the genealogy of other Shepard families, no one, of which we consider it probable, that Hannah, the wife of Joseph Blanchard, was a member.

8th.   The homesteads of the Blanchards and Shepards
were not far distant from each other.   Ralph Shepard's
house was situated in what was called "Bell Rock pasture,"
which was, probably, in the vicinity of what is known as
"Bell Rock burying ground," near which there is a station
on the Saugus branch of the Boston & Maine railroad.
This burying ground, and probably also the pasture here
referred to, took their names from the fact that a bell was
placed near there which, in the early settlement of the
town, was used to call the inhabitants to meeting.   The
house of Ralph Shepard, and a lot of land, of about four-
teen acres, which belonged to the homestead, was purchased
in 1666 by the Rev. Benjamin Bunker, a minister, who was
ordained in Malden, December 9, 1663, and who, at one
time, owned land in Charlestown, about Bunker Hill.   The
Shepard homestead is described as lying north of the parsonage and meeting-house lots, on both sides of "Penny
Ferry," which crossed the Mystic river, in the locality of
the present Malden bridge.

9th.   The location of the Blanchard and Shepard farms
made the families, for those times, neighbors.   They were

probably worshipers at the little meeting-house near Bell
Rock, where the children associated on Sundays, and, perhaps, they attended the same school, which may have been
the one which Ralph Shepard petitioned might be kept at
his house, but which petition was not granted. The marshes,
outstretching between Blanchard's Point and the home of
Ralph Shepard at Bell Rock, were only at times overflowed
with the tide water, which came up the Mystic river, and the
little estuaries, which may have run between the two places
here and there on the marsh land, would hardly form a
barrier, at low tide, to the neighborly visits of the two
families.

10th. Ralph Shepard, some time subsequent to 1663,
purchased a large land tract of six hundred and ten
acres, of Lieutenant Joseph Wheeler, of Concord, who
in turn received it from the government. This land
lay in the form of a triangle, according to Mr. Harwood,
the local historian, and was situated between the Indian
plantation of Nashoba, and what is now Westford. It is
stated, that in the tract of land, at or near the Elbridge
Marshall farm, was the home of Joseph Blanchard. " Nagog pond formed the base of the triangle, and the apex
was two miles one-quarter and sixty rods north from the
south-west end of Nagog pond, which would bring it to a
point on the Westford line, on or near the Deacon Man-
ning farm, but south of the road."

11th. A large part of the Shepard family moved to
the Littleton territory, and settled on land in the locality
of the paternal purchase; and among these was Walter
Powers the husband of Triall Shepard, who bought land of
his father-in-law, and took possession of it as early as 1666.

In view of these circumstances, we believe the fair inference is, that Joseph Blanchard married Hannah, a daughter
of Ralph Shepard, and that her name, like that of many
another member of a large family, in that busy and practical period of colonial life, was not placed on record, as
may have been the case with others of his children; and we
believe that the prime cause of Walter Powers' and Joseph
Blanchard's going to Littleton territory was the land purchase of their father-in-law, Ralph Shepard.

As undisputed tradition locates the birthplace of Calvin and Luther Blanchard on the farm now occupied by
Mr. Albert Littlefield of Boxboro, a short distance northerly
of the Boxboro railroad station, it may be that Simon, their
father, came into possession of this farm, either by inherit-
ance or purchase, and built upon it the house which originally stood there; or, it may be, that Joseph Blanchard, the
father of Simon and Jemima, moved from his early estate
on the Ralph Shepard purchase, and established a new
homestead on the farm afterwards occupied by Simon, and
where Luther and Calvin were born.

There is evidence of more than one of the Blanchard
family being early in Littleton territory; for, in the old
burying-ground of that town is, as we have noticed, a grave-
stone to John Blanchard, son of Thomas, who died October
10, 1745, aged nearly twenty-seven years.

As we have now traced the paternal and maternal ancestry of Calvin and Luther Blanchard to about the beginning of their history, as it is related to their Littleton
life, let us now notice something about the territory in
which they located.

The tract of country, in which the Blanchards and

Shepards lived, teemed with Indian reminiscences. It was once the home of Tahattawan, a chief of the Nashoba Indians, who, until the demoralization and devastation of Philip's war, lived in peaceful and pleasant occupation in a region whose sunny hillsides furnished abundant game, whose valleys and plain-lands furnished planting places for their corn, and where the little woodland lakelets of Nagog and Fort ponds supplied plenty of fish and wild water-fowl. Surely, Tahattawan and Pennakennit, who came after him, had ample reason for selecting such a place for a mission home; and as the blessed light of christianity was let in upon the hearts of these children of the woods, well may we suppose that its results were no less perceptible and benign, than the sunlight that came down through the treetops, on the deep forest shade. That this was so, history gives abundant evidence, for so manifest were the graces, as developed by the entrance of God's word, that the colonial authorities made good use of these christian Indians in negotiating with King Philip for the ransom of captives. Thomas Dublet, or Nepanet, was an agent in the release of Mrs. Rowlandson, who was captured at Lancaster, and was afterward ransomed near the foot of Wachuset mountain, Princeton, Mass., at or near a spot now marked by a memorial.

The wigwam of Thomas Dublet, tradition states, was near the Joel Proctor place. It is said that the fragment of a pot presented by Mr. Proctor, and supposed to have been Thomas Dublet's, is in the Reuben Hoar Library at Littleton. If the supposition concerning it is correct, the associations suggested by it are exceedingly interesting; for Sarah Dublet, the wife of Thomas, may many a time

have stood over it and stirred the savory contents of potted
venison, or pigeon or wild turkey, which was, perhaps, sea-
soned with sweet herbs, that grew in the garden plots of
the Powerses, the Shepards and the Blanchards, and were
generously granted her for the picking.   But the hearth of
Sarah's wigwam is cold, and from it the smoke no longer
curls upward through the treetops, indicatiug the presence
of an Indian abode.   In the act of incorporation of the
town of Littleton, in 1714, Sarah Dublet is supposed to
be referred to in the statement " And that Five hundred
Acres of Land be reserved and laid out for the Benefit of
any of the Descendants of the Indian Proprietors of the
Said Plantation that may be surviving; a Proportion thereof
to be for Sarah Dublet, alias Sarah Indian."   The reser-
vation thus made was the origin of the Littleton hamlet,
called Indian New-town.   Sarah Dublet, in 1734, was the
only heir to this five hundred acres, and old and decrepit,
she at length conveyed it to pay for her maintenance.

The original dwelling of the Blanchards was probably
constructed of logs, and the inmates were exposed to the
hardships of pioneer life in New England in the last part
of the seventeeth century ; and, probably, Joseph himself
frequently held such watch and ward over his possessions
as the times, made perilous by the predatory incursions of
the Northern and Eastern Indians, required for years after
the close of King Philip's war.   Doubtless the narration
of events, then recent, and the daring and fortitude ex-
hibited by his relatives, led Simon, the son of Joseph, and
father of Calvin and Luther, who was born October 5, 1728,
to enlist in his country's service.   But not only was the
neighborhood which was occupied by the Powerses, Shep-

ards and Blanchards rife with thrilling traditions, but it also contained landmarks and other objects that were rich in historic association.

Near Nashoba Hill, Walter Powers, an uncle of Joseph, erected, as is supposed, a " block house," the near neighborhood of which, if not the exact site, is still pointed out. The presence of this old garrison building, although in times of tranquility it was a mere defensive farmhouse, was suggestive of what was war-like, and of ominous reports of Indians, which had more than once sent the little households of the neighborhood from their warm firesides to this friendly stronghold for protection. But, probably, an event, which, more than any other, tended to make an impression upon Simon in his boyhood, was a sad mishap which befell three of the Shepard family, Isaac, Jacob and Mary, by which the two brothers lost their lives and the sister was captured. The event occurred on February 12, 1675–1676, just after the burning of Lancaster by the forces under King Philip. Isaac and Jacob Shepard were threshing grain in the barn, south of the house, on the south side of the lane to the present Pickard place, near the road. They had stationed their sister Mary, aged fifteen years, on Quagana hill, to watch for Indians, but she was taken by surprise and captured, her two brothers were killed, and the building was burned. Mary was taken away by the band of savages, but escaped the following night upon a horse, which the historian Hubbard states, was captured by the Indians the day before at Lancaster.

As the old Powers block-house and its neighborhood are closely associated with Calvin and Luther's ancestry,

they, perhaps, require more than a passing notice. The
house stood near Nashoba hill, and was long known as the
Reed house, because it was occupied later by Mr. Samuel
Reed. It was about a story and a half high, and had two
rooms on the ground floor, and two chambers or attic
rooms. It was destroyed by fire about 1828. The site of
the building, it is believed by the Littleton Historical
Society, has been nearly or quite definitely ascertained,
and that the house was undoubtedly built and originally
used by Walter Powers.

In the vicinity of the block-house is what was, probably, the first burying-ground of the early grantees. This
has been called the Powers burying-ground, and is said to
have contained an area of about eight rods by six. Years
ago, about a score of small rude grave-stones were visible,
standing about two feet out of the ground, having brief
inscriptions upon them. The bodies were buried with feet
toward a wall, which extended on one side of this burial
plot. In this ground, the body of Walter Powers was
undoubtedly interred; and it may have been originally set
apart by him as a family burial place, and perhaps most of
the bodies buried there, were of the Shepard, Powers, and
Blanchard households.

Several years ago a simple, natural stone was found in
the wall, near the premises, bearing the inscription, "W. P.,
1708," the day of the month, which was also given, corres-
ponding within two or three days with the date of Walter
Powers' death, in the Concord records. As other similar
stones, it is said, have been discovered thereabouts, it is
evident they were removed from the old graves by some

one who cleared this ancient burial place of the forefathers for the plow, which subsequently obliterated the mounds.

At what date this spot ceased to be used for interments is not known, but, as one of the earliest dates in the Littleton Common graveyard is 1717 or 1718, and no stone bears the name of Powers or Shepard, and but three bear the name of Blanchard, we conclude that the little, lone spot, east of the hollow by the wall, contains the dust of those ancient householders, but this region, once so identified with these three family names, long since ceased to hear them spoken, except as belonging to parties living elsewhere. Other families have taken their places; not a furrow in a Littleton field is now turned by a Blanchard; not an acre is tilled by a Powers or a Shepard, but the whole range of territory, from the old garrison-house, through "Newton" or "Newtowne," where Thomas Blanchard owned meadow land, to the Albert Littlefield farm, the early home of Calvin and Luther, is now trodden by stranger footsteps, and inhabited by those not to the ancient "manor born." The little plot, which probably contains what is mortal of the pioneer grantees of the 17th century, alone keeps its treasure, notwithstanding that which indicated its whereabouts has been so unfortunately removed, as if the living begrudged the resting places of the dead. But even this little which remains will yet waste; and not until the great resurrection morning, will that be restored which will give a semblance of the prime actors who have long been silent. But, though dead, their influence, and the results of what they did is still active. The present is a product of a busy past, and while the old woodland walls have tumbled, and the loose stones lie

moss-grown in the shrubbery, and the land ranges have become indistinct, yet the greater community that has come
in, with its improved schools and more comfortable homesteads, are but the outgrowth of the noble efforts of those
who, by their sturdy toil, thus early staked out their claims
and established their rude boundary lines.

Not only did Joseph, the younger, live in a period in
which the events and traditions connected with Philip's
war were fresh, but he lived when he himself was an actor
in stirring scenes of a similar character. It was the first
quarter of the Eighteenth century when the drear wood-
lands again rang with the savage shout, and the fair intervals were again to be fought over by the settlers. The foe
might at any time be seen in his doorway, or he might at
any time discover signs of lurking savages, who were
lying in wait to kill or capture their victims and
burn his dwelling. The sound of a musket fired in the far
off forest, an unusual smoke rising upward on the hazy
horizon, the strange imprint of a moccasined foot in the
soft meadow land, the return from the pasture path of a
wounded cow, a herd of deer fleeing affrighted through
the clearing, all of these might be omens that betokened
danger, and rendered the ordinary life of Joseph Blanchard
one of watchfulness and suspense.

This was the period of the daring ranger expeditions
which called for a sagacity and military prowess that were
exceptional. In this service Joseph's own townspeople
and kinsmen were engaged. In one of these expeditions
Ephraim Powers, with seventeen others were attacked
by Indians, while on the march from Northfield to Fort
Dummer. Jonathan Lawrence, a comrade of Powers, was

captured and taken to Canada. Powers was stripped, robbed of his firearms and wounded in the head. In the ill-starred expedition of Lieut.-Col. John Winslow to Nova Scotia, in 1755, were several soldiers from Littleton, among whom were David and Walter Powers, husbandmen. This is the expedition that took the French Neutrals, so called, from their pleasant homes in Arcadia, which event the poet Longfellow has made pathetically prominent in his poem, "Evangeline." Some of the neutrals, who were removed, were brought to Littleton. They are called on the town records, "Neuters." This unfortunate class was billeted out among the towns of the Bay Province, and were the wards of the places to which they were assigned. Thus was the age and environment of Simon Blanchard's father of a nature suited to stamp its impress upon the children; and it is no wonder that when the last of the dark and eventful intercolonial wars between England and France set in, Simon, who was born October 6, 1728, should enlist in that perilous service, which brought the soldier face to face with, perhaps, one of the worst combinations of men that ever engaged in civilized warfare; a mongrel element of Indians, French and halfbreeds. As the conflict waged by the English was mainly by expeditions into a cold, rough country, the hardship was unusually severe. We conclude Simon was in several expeditions.

His name is among a list of men certified to, September 27, 1755, belonging to Col. Josiah Brown's regiment; as engaged in the expedition against Crown Point. (State Archieves, vol. 93, page 206). His name is also on a muster-roll, dated Boston, March 4, 1758, of a company under

command of Captain Daniel Fletcher. Entered service
September 15; served until September 30. (State Archives,
vol. 94, page 71). He is also spoken of in connection with
the Crown Point expedition, year not given, but probably
1755; reported sick at home.

His last and crowning act of service was at the capture
of Quebec, which took place December 17, 1759. This
place was captured by General Wolf and his daring army
of English and colonial soldiers, who made their way up a
narrow pathway above the St. Lawrence river, and at early
morning surprised Montcalm, the French commander, on
the plains of Abraham. In the conflict that ensued General Wolf fell, with many of his triumphant followers, and
among these was Simon Blanchard.

In this connection a few facts may be interesting relative to the expedition that Calvin engaged in, to take from
the English the same capital city of Canada, that his father,
but a few years before, helped them to conquer from the
French. This expedition started in September, 1775. It
is thus described by the historian Quackenbos: "No one
can estimate the hardships that devoted band were called
on to endure; now forcing their way through tangled
thickets and over pathless mountains; and now wading
through swollen rivers, pushing their boats before them, or
borne away by rapids and struggling for life amid the
waves; worn out, sick, cold, hungry, disheartened. Not a
few gave up the expedition, and returned to Massachusetts.
With some of his bravest men, Arnold pushed on to a
French village for supplies, leaving the rest of his force in
a most critical position. The last ox was killed and dis-
tributed; the last dog was eaten with avidity; then roots

and moose-skin moccasins were their only resource. When the aid sent back by Arnold reached the famished band, they had eaten nothing for two days. Even such suffering, however, could not discourage these brave hearts."

In 1760, administration papers were granted for the settlement of the estate of Simon Blanchard. One of the sureties on the probate bond was Sarah, the widow of Joseph Blanchard. According to the inventory filed the estate was appraised as follows: Real estate, 160 £; personal property, 62 £ 16s 6d; total 212 £ 16s 6d. Among the assets was given the following item: "And also wages due for his services done His Majesty at Quebec, 29 £ 1s." Among the charges the first item was: "To mourning for herself and children." From the report of the appraisers, relative to the real property, we are led to infer that Simon Blanchard's farm was adjacent to lands of his father, for they give the boundary lines on the northwesterly and southwesterly, as lying along "land and meadow of Joseph Blanchard." The children being minors, guardians were appointed for them. Joseph Worster serving for Calvin, and Ephraim Hosmer for Luther. According to tradition, a portion, at least, of the home farm passed into the hands of Calvin, born February 27, 1754. Calvin married Abigail Reed of Westford. They had nine children, among whom was Simon, who was born in Boxboro, April 3, 1784. As the oldest son, Calvin, kept the homeplace, Simon went to Littleton, where he learned the cooper's trade of Joseph Fletcher. After working at his trade seven years he married Martha Shattuck, a descendant of Rev. Benjamin Shattuck, first minister of Littleton. They had two children. October 27, 1814, Simon married for his second wife, Mary, daughter of Joseph and Sarah Keyes of Westford. They were the parents of nine children, among whom was Luke, the third son.

LUKE BLANCHARD.

A memorial volume, commemorative of Calvin and Luther Blanchard would, perhaps, hardly be complete without a short, biographical sketch of the publisher.

Luke Blanchard was born in Boxboro, January 17, 1826. His early life was spent on his father's farm, and, like most country children, he was busily occupied with such work as a boy could do, and received but scanty school privileges. At the age of eleven he commenced driving an ox-team to Boston; a work which tended to test his patience, and by the vicissitudes of the weather, to test also the strength of his physique.

The boy successfully endured the tests, and at the age of twenty-one, after having attended school at Nashua, N. H., one term, he started out for himself as a dealer in country produce, which business he has successfully pursued up to the present time. Besides conducting an extensive commission trade in country produce, he has dealt extensively in real property, and is also engaged in the lumber business. His landed possessions are situated in several of the states, and also in the British provinces.

The commission office and headquarters of the Blanchards are at No. 20, Quincy Market, South Market street, Boston, where Luke Blanchard, with his son, Arthur F., born January 21, 1864, do business under the firm name of L. Blanchard and Company.

Mr. Luke Blanchard married Miss Jerusha Vose, April 8, 1858. They are the parents of four children, two of whom are living. Each of the surviving children reside at West Acton. Anna is a member of her father's household. Arthur married Miss Charlotte T. Sanderson, daughter of Hon. George W. Sanderson of Littleton, January 28, 1891.

Mr. Blanchard is, for a person of his age, in fairly good health, and conducts his business with the zest and carefulness of former years. Being a pioneer in apple exportation, he has continued to interest himself in the business, not only by employing his capital, but by giving it his personal supervision. Thus we conclude, that the ancestors' traits have been transmitted to, and had development in their descendants; and the act of Luke Blanchard, in endeavoring to perpetuate the memory of his worthy sires, may be considered as a thankoffering to them, and a reminder to posterity of the source, under Providence, of whatever prosperity they may be permitted to enjoy.

LUTHER BLANCHARD'S DEATH.

VIII.

Wondrous and awful are thy silent halls,
    O, kingdom of the past !
There lie the bygone ages in their palls,
    Guarded by shadows vast,—

       *   *   *   *

Thy mighty clamors, wars and world noised deeds
    Are silent now in dust,
Gone like a tremble of the huddling reeds
    Beneath some sudden gust.

       *   *   *   *

Here 'mid the bleak waves of our strife and care,
    Float the green Fortunate Isles
Where all thy hero spirits dwell, and share
    Our martyrdoms and toils.
                          James Russell Lowell.

As we close this brief history of Luther Blanchard, it may be appropriate to consider some things relative to the cause of his death.

The inscription on the memorial stone states, that "Luther was the first man hit by a British bullet at the old North Bridge, and died in the service of his country a few months later." This inscription, according to oft repeated and well authenticated tradition, might be supplemented by, From the effects of the wound. That this tradition may have its full force and effect, we submit the following considerations:

1st. When there is no evidence against a proposition or statement which is not only possible but highly probable, it takes but little evidence to establish it.

2d. When the truth of a proposition or statement is possible and highly probable, and there is a strong presumption in its favor, it takes much evidence to overthrow it.

When these rules are applied in the case before us, the fact that Luther Blanchard, the young Acton fifer, died of the wound received at Concord, stands out distinctly and in a way to challenge rebuttal. To begin with, we believe it safe to assert that there is no authority, either of tradition or of record, for assigning his death to any other cause; neither, to our knowledge, has such authority ever been quoted, or found its way into public print. If there have been any doubts, they have, so far as we are informed, been unaccompanied by substantial reasons therefor, and have arisen rather from the absence of any official report relative to the cause of Luther Blanchard's death, than from one scrap of evidence that the cause was other than tradition declares it to be.

To consider closely the main features of this subject, let us notice the two general sources from which history springs. These are, first, tradition as to things remote, and living heresay as to things intermediate and in the near past; secondly, the data or dictum of records written or printed.

In the instance before us, when we turn to these two sources, we find on the one hand tradition ample in quantity, and trustworthy in quality; and on the other, such sufficient reasons for any absence or omission of records, written or printed, as might satisfy any inquirer for the facts. As to the information that has come to us from tradition, it is substantial, simple and natural. It comes from families and from citizens whose patriotic fervor has been undoubted, whose integrity none may question, and whose opportunity to know has been good.

That the traditions concerning Luther Blanchard's death have mainly come from his own family is only natural, and what under the circumstances might be expected. Had he died only a few hours after receiving his wound, as was the case with James Hayward, his death would have been so closely connected with its cause, that the two events would as a matter of common knowledge hardly have been separated. The whole tragedy being almost in one simultaneous and single act, the tidings of it would be as of one event, and would naturally be told in the simple statement, He was shot and soon died. But under the circumstances attending the death of Luther Blanchard, this could hardly be expected, for it was an instance involving weeks and months, with all the intermediary incidents and episodes in that epoch making period, from the retreat of the Regulars April 19th, to the fierce conflict at Bunker Hill, June 17th. The chronological space was altogether too long, and the complication of perils was too great for the detailed experience of a wounded soldier to be followed by the public through camp and field and hospital, till he was reported on the muster rolls " dead." There were no town " war committees " then, to as carefully note things as in our Civil War; it was a time when each family was left mainly to keep the record of its own soldier members.

The siege of Boston was one of prolonged and perilous vicissitude. During its continuance there were enlistments and re-enlistments ; families were decimated, households were broken up, lands abandoned and left in barrenness. It was enough for each family and hamlet to know that their own loved ones were spared, and if others went forth and died, they would hardly stop to consider the cause of their death. In the time of our country's early wars, town records were few and scant, and even complete lists of the greater casualties were, if obtained, not always preserved. But the records of communities and of mere neighborhoods, and much the more of single households, were still more fragmentary and scant. Stationery was scarce, the king's stamp upon paper was a mark of detestation to an incensed, tax-oppressed people, and but little patronage would the royal revenue receive from the patriotic householder, even by the scant purchase of a piece of crown paper, upon which to preserve a brief family record. Even in our own day, few are they who have a written record of family casualties in the late Civil War. Their reliance is on the sad inscriptions written on their hearts or upon the public records of the state or nation.

Small opportunity, therefore, was there for the public at large to be apprised at once of the cause of Luther

Blanchard's death. They might know by the military rolls that he died; but when he died, and of what, few would stop to investigate or even to inquire. Not so with the family. Although the age was such a practical one, and the sentimental side of things was so often ignored, and from sheer necessity it had to give way to the more substantial, there, nevertheless, were tenderly cherished in the memory of households the choice annals of each life history, and the details and causes of events that brought bereavement and loss. Leading events were remembered and rehearsed to the children and the children's children, until, like the ballads and legends of the old Scottish minstrels, they at length became engrafted upon society, and finally crystalized into national history. So it was in the instance of this conspicuous actor in the American Revolution.

As the echo of the shots that were fired, responsive to those which hit the youthful musician and those others, whose names like his have immortalized the annals of Acton, died away, and the smoke, mingling with the morning mists of the river and the meadows, rose upward and faded, so the details of the conflict and a portion of the sequel, as these affected only the individual actor and his family, were lost sight of by the public in the great din and dreadfulness of the scenes of that memorable year between April 19, 1775 and March 17, 1776, when the last English man-of-war left the Massachusetts Bay waters. But, little by little, the facts through tradition have come to the front, and so may they continue to become prominent until honor is given to whom honor is due, and standard history incorporates with our nation's leading events these interesting family annals.

In view, then, of the exceptional nature of the times, and the consequent obscurity of the circumstances attending Luther Blanchard's death, it is not strange that the public was not apprised of its cause; nor that it should fail to be known other than by family tradition, nor readily pass into history. Neither is it a matter of wonder that the Provincial war records failed to give the cause of his death; it was for these to give the fact of his death; for the recording officer to do more than this, might, under the circumstances, be going beyond his province; for Luther Blanchard, it is alleged, died from a wound received at the Concord fight, and not from a cause incident to any service in the Continental army. When he was struck by the British bullet, he was a minute-man, and as such, as we have seen, was doing a quasi independent service. After he arrived at Charlestown, his work as a minute-man ended; at that time he began a new service, and entered by a new enlistment that organization called the Continental army, for eight months' service, designed for the siege of Boston. As, then, the wound causing his death was received prior to this later enlistment, nothing, perhaps, should be expected from the Continental army records, except the words found there, "Reported dead." But when we turn to the true and natural chronicler of personal events, and search the only source of history that can be expected to preserve and transmit them, we hear the utterance of unmistakable voices. Then it is, that we have testimony that should be unquestioned as to its trustworthiness, because they who gave it were honest and competent witnesses. It has never been a matter of doubt by members of the Blanchard family of Boxboro or Acton that Luther died from the wound received at the Concord North bridge, although, no one ever pretended to give the exact time.

Among those who have made the oft-repeated and positive declaration that Luther died of his North bridge wound, was Calvin, his brother, who, being also at the siege of Boston, until he went on the Canada expedition in September, was in a position to know whether or not that wound was ever healed ; and, moreover, on his return from Canada, he could easily ascertain if it caused his death. Calvin Blanchard always stated in unequivocal terms that his brother Luther died from the effects of that wound ; and, repeatedly, did his son Simon state what he had so often heard from his father's lips about his uncle Luther.

We would state here, that if the value of tradition is to be rated by the grade of character of those who communicate it, it is entitled in this case to a high estimate; for Simon Blanchard was a most estimable citizen, and a man unusually careful and considerate in speech ; what he heard and believed, he repeated just as it was, and transmitted to posterity only what he sincerely and earnestly believed. In an interview with a citizen of Acton concerning the cause of Luther Blanchard's death, he informed us that Mr. Simon Blanchard told him when a boy, that his father said his uncle Luther died of a wound received at the Concord fight. Mr. Luke Blanchard, son of Simon, says that his father was always positive in stating that his father told him that his brother Luther died of the wound received at Concord. Thus has the tradition come down through the one natural channel whence such information usually passes into the future. By such rills the great river of history gathers and widens and flows, until it becomes a mighty stream and landmark of time at which they who thirst for a knowledge of the past, stop and drink. Much of standard history is received from tales told first by the hearthstone or by the group seated by the country-side, or uttered, it may be, at the crossroads store, or at the village inn.

Once exclude that portion of our country's chronicles, which has come down through private channels, and many of our choice annals would be lost. But it is unnecessary to dwell longer on the evidence upon which this interesting fact rests, for we believe enough has already been stated to substantiate every claim that has been made for the youthful fifer.

Before closing, however, we would state, that every presumption in the premises perhaps favors what the testimony here adduced or reviewed tends to establish. Each statement made about the cause of Luther Blanchard's death, which stands collaterally related to the main issue, or which as an episode stands related to the main fact, is corroborative of it. The assertion that has often been made, that Luther Blanchard died in a building of Harvard College, then used as a hospital, coupled with the assertion that he died of the wound received at the old North bridge, is a coincidence of statements, which we believe makes probable all that is alleged in each, for naturally the two traditions, being thus connected, stand or fall together. That Harvard College was used as a barrack, and hence presumably as a place for any sick soldier, is a fact established in history, being given in a history of Harvard College and also in the history of Middlesex County, published by Lewis and Company, in 1890, vol. 1, page 89. In the latter volume, it is stated, that in April 1775, when the Massachusetts militia was concentrated at Cambridge, the college government removed the library and apparatus to Andover, and a little later, ordered it to be removed to Concord. The legislature was afterwards applied to for indemnification for damage done by the soldiers, when they occupied the building, and for loss of rent.

If the statement that Luther Blanchard died of any wound is correct, the circumstances are such as lead almost conclusively to a belief that it was the one received at the North bridge; for there was but little opportunity for him to receive a wound anywhere else, without its being recorded, and without its being known to his brother. It is not claimed that his name is on the list of casualties at Bunker Hill. In the siege of Boston there was little, if any skirmishing of a nature that much imperilled the American ranks, and no battle was fought there after June 17th. As late as August 1st, the name of Luther Blanchard, with the rank of corporal, is on the muster rolls. This leads to the presumption that he was able-bodied at that time and without any serious injury at the battle of Bunker Hill. That he died of disease is, in the presence of the slightest testimony that he died of a wound, hardly admissible for a moment.

We are informed he was a man of fine physique, athletic and powerful. The Middlesex contingent of the continental army was operating on its native heath, and there were no unusual perils of climate to be encountered. Thus

it is, that every circumstance and tradition concur in declaring that Luther Blanchard's death was from a wound
made by a British musket ball at the North bridge,
Concord, Mass., April 19th, 1775. It is unnecessary to
explain any silence of history concerning this matter prior
to the last quarter-century. History is not always complete until years after the occurrences which it relates.
Length of time is a great revealer of what has transpired
within its mysterious cycles. History shrinks and gathers
and grows again as successive resurrections disclose the
false and declare the true. As men come and men go,
they leave at last the world's annals in the hands of those,
who in an unprejudiced way, and unwarped by the petty
influences of locality and personality, do justice to its
actors. Then, history arrives at its best, then, if ever, it
is finished.

Not until tradition could be given its right place; not
until there was set upon it a fair appraisal; not until beliefs
were built upon evidence, rather than upon the absence
of it, was Luther Blanchard given his merited place in the
annals of the Revolutionary war.

As to how it occurred that Luther Blanchard, after
receiving a fatal bullet wound at the old North bridge,
April 19th, could continue in military service, and meanwhile pass through the fierce conflict at Bunker Hill, and
the rigor of camp life, and of work in the intrenchments
about Boston, and succumb afterwards to its effects, is not
for us to explain. We are called upon to deal with the
evidence of facts, not to formulate theories as to a reason
for their existence, nor to offer explanations regarding
their relations. The question is, Did he die as tradition

has alleged? Not, How came he to die thus? But, if no ready explanation could be given, it might be dealing unfairly with evidence, and impair the rights of the truth, to doubt the credibility of witnesses, because we cannot readily explain what they testify to.

Life is full of strange mysteries, and great is the mystery of living, and the history of human transactions is not always complete in its philosophy, nor clear as to the processes that evolve the facts it preserves; yet the province of history is not impaired by this, nor its accumulations and conclusions discredited. But, although not called for, it is by no means difficult to conjecture how it happened with Luther Blanchard. It is not hard to suppose that a wound might terminate fatally, which, for a season, gave but little discomfort. Repeatedly in the surgical reports of the war department are such instances doubtless recorded, even in modern times, with all the improved methods for the removal of gunshots and the prevention of subsequent mischief. But a century or more ago, surgery was, as compared with its present perfected condition, near its infancy; and a bullet, fitting the bore of a British musket, lodged in or passing through a human body, or even slightly injuring it, may easily be conceived to occasion mischief months afterwards, under adverse conditions, such as an exposure to the elements, hard service and neglect. That these conditions existed there can be little doubt. Military life, at its best, is wearing to the soldier in the ranks. The gloss and coloring of a dress parade, and the gay glamour of a gala occasion in times of peace are but faint hints of what war is. War is war, although it be in one's own neighborhood, and where many of its asperities can be softened by the best ministrations of friends and a grateful country. So, doubtless, Luther Blanchard found it in the camp at Winter Hill, which locality in those days was, perhaps, bleak in winter, and in summer exposed in bald barrenness to the hot rays of a New England sun. Moreover, Luther Blanchard was not the soldier to shirk; the stern spirit of his ancestors, that sent Calvin through the Kennebec wilds into Canada, and his father before him to Quebec, doubtless prompted him to his best endeavor, and led him to hold out in the camp, till further persistence was impossible.

Our conjecture based upon the foregoing conclusions is, that the ball which hit Luther Blanchard struck him in a manner that left him free of limb to march and to fife ; and that when he enlisted at Cambridge for an eight months' service as a Continental soldier, he was comparatively robust and strong ; but that the wound received April 19th, from complicated conditions and agencies while in camp, became active and acute, and finally proved fatal. Such a conjecture explains all that is necessary, and is consistent with what is claimed in this history.

www.ingramcontent.com/pod-product-compliance
Lightning Source LLC
Chambersburg PA
CBHW022142020726
47496CB00008B/2513